WILL THE *REAL* SARA STANLEY
PLEASE COME FORWARD

Sara felt Jo's envy keenly. She reddened, embarrassed to have so many worldly goods when Jo obviously had so little.

Felix, however, was looking at Jo as she paraded before the mirror in Sara's finery. "I can't believe how much you two look like sisters!" he remarked.

"Really?" said Sara, taking a long look at Jo herself. "You think so?"

All at once, they heard the door slam below and Felicity's voice calling out from downstairs. "Felix...? Sara...? Are you up there?"

An impish grin lit up Felix's face. "Jo, you go down!" he whispered impulsively, "It's my nosy sister, see if you can fool her into thinking you're Sara."

"Don't be silly, Felix," hissed Sara. "Felicity's smart, she'll guess right off!"

"Betcha she won't," said Jo, her eyes gleaming.

Sara stared at Jo. They *did* look alike ... and it would be such a lark to pull the wool over Felicity's eyes for once!

**Also available in the Road to Avonlea Series
from Bantam Skylark books**

But When She Was Bad...

Storybook written by

Marlene Matthews

Based on the Sullivan Films Production
written by Marlene Matthews
adapted from the novels of

Lucy Maud Montgomery

A BANTAM SKYLARK BOOK®
NEW YORK · TORONTO · LONDON · SYDNEY · AUCKLAND

Based on the Sullivan Films Production produced by Sullivan Films Inc.
in association with CBC and the Disney Channel with the participation
of Telefilm Canada adapted from Lucy Maud Montgomery's novels.

Teleplay written by Marlene Matthews
Copyright © 1991 by Sullivan Films Distribution, Inc.

This edition contains the complete text
of the original edition.
NOT ONE WORD HAS BEEN OMITTED.

RL 6, 008–012

BUT WHEN SHE WAS BAD...
A Bantam Skylark Book / published by arrangement with
HarperCollins Publishers Ltd.

PUBLISHING HISTORY
HarperCollins edition published 1994
Bantam edition / July 1994

ROAD TO AVONLEA is the trademark of Sullivan Films Inc.

Skylark Books is a registered trademark of Bantam Books,
a division of Bantam Doubleday Dell Publishing Group, Inc.
Registered in U.S. Patent and Trademark Office and elsewhere.

ISBN 0-553-48122-3

Bantam Books are published by Bantam Books, a division of Bantam Doubleday Dell
Publishing Group, Inc. Its trademark, consisting of the words "Bantam Books" and the
portrayal of a rooster, is Registered in U.S. Patent and Trademark Office and in other
countries. Marca Registrada. Bantam Books, 1540 Broadway, New York, New York 10036.

PRINTED IN THE UNITED STATES OF AMERICA
OPM 0 9 8 7 6 5 4 3 2 1

Chapter One

"It isn't fair," Sara muttered to herself, her blue eyes storming with indignation as she set the silverware on the table. "No matter what I do, she treats me just like a baby!"

Sara didn't dare say the words aloud. Not with Aunt Hetty peering at her from across the kitchen, itching to find fault with her work. At that very moment she was scrutinizing the dinner table like a maitre d' at the Ritz.

"Forks on the left, Sara Stanley, knives on the right," dictated Hetty, gesturing with a half-peeled potato in her hand. "Dinner fork, then salad fork, *then* the plate and *then* the knives."

"I've set the table a million times, Aunt Hetty, I know where things go without being told!" Sara gritted her teeth and waited for the retort that was certain to follow...a *humph!* and then a sharp *sniff*. But she was wrong—this time the *sniff* came first, followed by the famous *humph!*

No *sniff* and *humph!* in the world sounded quite like Hetty King's. Grown men quaked in their boots and small children shivered at the sound. Even though Uncle Alec always said Hetty's bark was worse than her bite, Sara knew better. Hetty's bark hurt, and Sara had the bruised feelings to prove it.

"The forks are crooked," Hetty observed. "They must be lined up properly. Cutlery should march across the table like soldiers."

Sara groaned. Who cared if the forks marched like soldiers? Who but Aunt Hetty would even notice? Still, she obeyed, moving the forks an exact quarter of an inch.

"Now the knives," ordered Aunt Hetty. "Line them up to match."

"But…" Sara began.

"No buts. Crooked cutlery makes the table look sloppy, and a sloppy table is a sign of a sloppy mind." With that, Hetty returned to her potatoes. Each brown peel curled into a perfect spiral, and each potato emerged spotlessly pure and white and was placed in a bowl of cold water to soak until dinnertime.

With a sigh, Sara rearranged the knives so they were in step with the forks. You'd think the King of England dined at Rose Cottage, the way Aunt Hetty fussed over every tiny detail. And it was only herself and Aunt Hetty for dinner these days, now that Aunt Olivia and Jasper Dale were married, with their own table to set in their honeymoon cottage. Sara was certain Aunt Olivia wouldn't natter at her if the forks weren't just so. Neither would Aunt Janet…nor anyone else, for that matter.

Wistfully, she gazed out the open window. Beyond Rose Cottage were golden fields that beckoned invitingly, and nodding buttercups and tall grasses rippled gracefully in the summer breeze. A breath of salt air hinted of the sea, of sailing ships and romantic adventures in exotic, foreign lands. Sara ached to fling the door open and run...to someplace, any place, far from the confines of Aunt Hetty's strict kitchen.

When Sara had first come to Avonlea, it was in the company of her Nanny Louisa. Sara's mother was dead, and her father was unable to care for her because he had to fight to save his business and his good name against false accusations. Back then, to Sara, this beautiful island where her mother had grown up seemed positively idyllic. She had never lived in such a pretty, peaceful place. Here she would be embraced and loved by the only family left to her, her aunts, uncles and cousins. And Aunt Hetty, as the eldest of the King clan, would be her guardian.

True, Aunt Hetty had been difficult from the start. She and Nanny Louisa had locked horns instantly, bickering over everything from how to boil water to the correct way to thread a darning needle. Sara remembered Nanny glaring at Aunt Hetty and whispering a word of warning to her young charge: "Mark my words, Sara, leopards do not change their spots."

Sara was very fond of her Aunt Hetty, but she'd had to admit that Nanny Louisa was right. Aunt Hetty would never change, not one bit. And now that Sara was twelve years old, practically grown up, she longed to be treated differently. After all, her cousin Felicity, who was scarcely older than Sara, was given much more respect and all sorts of privileges at home. More and more these days, Sara struggled under Aunt Hetty's thumb and dreamed of freedom.

Once upon a time she had travelled, in the company of her beloved father, to all the great cities of the world—London, Paris, Rome. But after her father died in an accident, she'd put aside her memories of those long-ago adventures, and now they seemed like nothing more than a dream. The more Aunt Hetty sniped at her, though, the more she had begun to yearn once again for that world beyond Avonlea.

In the stillness of the night, she would lie awake in bed watching airy moonbeams filter through lace curtains, and while the wind howled in the eaves outside Rose Cottage, she would conjure up the images of that faraway life. They were like the memories of some long-ago princess on a gilded throne...the elegant dining rooms in the grand hotels of Europe, where the forks and knives were handled by white-gloved waiters who hovered, serving pâté and pheasant under glass. Hotel staff would bow to her handsome father and cater to his every whim: "Mr. Stanley, may we present you with an orchid for your lovely daughter?" "Mr. Stanley, the air is rather chilly this evening, would you care for a fur robe for your daughter's knees?"

"For heaven's sake, Sara Stanley, have you gone stone deaf? Answer the door!"

Aunt Hetty's sharp voice shattered Sara's reverie. Cheeks aflame, she made a beeline for the front door.

"How ya doin', Sara? Miss King home? I brung my homework for her to check." It was Gus Pike standing there, grinning broadly. Behind him was Sara's cousin, Felicity King, with a basket over her arm. Before Sara could answer, Felicity swept past both of them and into the kitchen, where she unpacked the basket, lifting out fragrant raspberry tarts and retrieving a small jar, which she handed to Hetty.

"Aunt Hetty, I baked these tarts this morning…oh, and here's some wonderful furniture polish I discovered in Cavendish last week. I did all the furniture in the parlor for mother and she just adored it!"

"Why, thank you, Felicity, that was very thoughtful of you," said Hetty as she unscrewed the jar and smelled the fresh pine scent of the polish. "Your mother is lucky to have a little homemaker like you."

Felicity flushed with pleasure at the compliment. Sara drew back, strangely quiet. Why did Aunt Hetty bubble over with praise for anything Felicity did but had nothing but criticism for Sara?

Adding insult to injury, Hetty quickly looked over the papers Gus handed her and then glanced up and smiled warmly. "Good work, Gus!" She cast Sara a reproachful glance. "Take a lesson, Sara Stanley. I gave Gus this assignment yesterday and here it is done…and done extremely well, I might add!"

As if reading Sara's mind, Gus shuffled his feet and said, "Aw, Sara's got chores to do at home, Miss King, and I ain't got no home so I got plenty o' time on my hands, there's the difference."

"Don't go making excuses for Sara," scoffed Aunt Hetty, "she's got an easy row to hoe compared to you. Why, she couldn't handle a job at the cannery and get her schoolwork done on time if her life depended on it!"

Sara reddened with shame. She always did her homework...except for the few times when she forgot...oh, and once when she fell asleep daydreaming over a book of poetry...and of course the time when Felix threw her notebook into a bonfire by mistake, but that didn't count because it wasn't her fault. Still, how could Aunt Hetty embarrass her in front of Gus and Felicity like this? It was so humiliating!

Hetty plunged on, oblivious to Sara's discomfort. "I do hope Sara will be responsible like the two of you when she grows up!"

"I *am* grown up!" retorted Sara, but she might as well have spoken to the wall for all the good it did.

"You're only twelve," purred Felicity, from the lofty height of her fourteen years. She thoroughly enjoyed this chance to lord it over Sara. "But don't worry, you'll improve with age. Don't you think she will, Gus?"

"Uh...well, sure, I suppose..." muttered Guy, concerned for Sara's feelings. "Say, we're headin' over by the bridge, Sara. Come on fishin' with us! I got a batch o' big fat worms, real fresh ones."

Sara flashed a grateful smile at Gus, but before she could open her mouth to say yes, Hetty uttered a sharp "No."

"But why? I'm finished setting the table, Aunt Hetty. Can't I go...please?"

"I said no. We are going shopping. Olivia is meeting us at the general store in exactly fifteen minutes."

"But I don't want to go shopping, I want to go fishing," pleaded Sara.

"Young lady, you have outgrown all your dresses, and I don't intend to keep Olivia waiting."

"I simply adore shopping for clothes," murmured Felicity, knowing full well she was adding fuel to the fire. "Mrs. Lawson just received a new shipment of the most darling things! I'd be excited if I were you, Sara."

"Clearly, she isn't you, or she'd be more appreciative," was Aunt Hetty's dry comment. "Run along now. Sara won't be joining you today."

Sara hung back. It was useless. She felt like a puppet, a silly puppet without a thought in her head that Aunt Hetty didn't tell her to think. Sara was sure she'd be old and gray and Aunt Hetty would still be pulling the strings, telling her what to do and when to do it.

As if reading her thoughts, Gus smiled kindly. "Hey, don't worry none, Sara. The fish ain't gonna stop bitin', we'll go another day. So long, Miss King." Gus ushered Felicity out the door. He felt badly, but he knew how stubborn Hetty King could be. There was precious little he could do to comfort Sara.

Chapter Two

Aunt Hetty sat ramrod stiff beside a silent Sara as the buggy rattled along the road to Avonlea. The moment they pulled up to the general store, however, Sara's eyes widened in surprise.

There it was...*the* dress...the most unbelievable dress, hanging in solitary splendor in the store window. In a twinkling, her reluctance to go shopping simply vanished.

It was destiny.

Rose colored, like the first faint blush of dawn, the dress was a vision of sheer crêpe-de-chine, ruffled and bowed and exquisite. It spoke to her of the couturiers in Paris where Nanny Louisa had once ordered all her clothes. Sara hadn't thought of such finery in ages...but there it was, utter, rosy perfection, simply begging to be bought.

"Good Lord, child, what are you gawking at?" demanded Hetty as she clambered out of the buggy and hurried towards the store. Olivia waved to them through the store window.

"That!" breathed Sara, enraptured, one hand clutched to her heart while the other pointed towards the window. Rows of delicate pleating cascaded from a high, embroidered neckline festooned with roses of silk and lace. A pale-pink velvet sash, encrusted with seed pearls and silk bows, looped around the empire waist, trailing wispy garlands of tiny bejeweled flowers.

Hetty glanced briefly at the object of Sara's affection. Up went an eyebrow, followed by the *humph!* and *sniff*.

"Don't dawdle, Sara, Aunt Olivia's already here." With that, Hetty swept into the store without so much as a backward glance at the rosy wonder in the window.

Tearing her gaze from the dress, Sara practically stumbled over her own feet, dropping the little beaded purse that held her birthday money from Nanny Louisa. Quickly she scooped it up and followed Hetty King inside.

The store was crowded with the usual mixture of Avonlea patrons. Some were shoppers who dawdled and others were dawdlers who shopped. Those who paused in their shopping and their dawdling did so to gossip, to see and be seen, and to keep tabs on the comings and goings of the busy little community.

Mrs. Potts and Mrs. Bugle were picking and pawing through a new shipment of corsets, which classified them as shoppers. But they slipped into the dawdler category because they had long since made their purchases and were lingering in order to ascertain just why Olivia Dale was chit-chatting with Mrs. Lawson about a certain length of expensive, pale-blue watered silk.

"She certainly doesn't need another dress! Olivia Dale has more clothes than a dog has fleas," whispered Mrs. Potts, casting a knowing look at Mrs. Bugle.

"If you ask me," Mrs. Bugle whispered back, "she's spending far too much of her husband's money. Though I can't say I blame her. Must be a relief after living with a penny-pincher like Hetty King."

"Well, speak of the devil," hissed Mrs. Potts, with a nudge and a nod towards the door.

Both women fell silent and pretended to

busy themselves with some lace petticoats as Hetty swept into the store, with Sara tagging along behind her. Olivia glanced up and smiled a welcome, holding the blue watered silk up under her chin and posing prettily.

"Hetty...Sara...What do you think? Should I buy it? It's Jasper's favorite shade of blue."

Mrs. Potts and Mrs. Bugle dropped the petticoats and edged closer to eavesdrop.

"Oh, do take it, Aunt Olivia!" cried Sara. "It matches your eyes perfectly!"

"Nonsense," snapped Hetty, peering down her nose at her sister. "A wishy-washy color like that shows every drop of dirt. You'll be sorry you wasted your money on such foolishness."

Olivia smiled wryly. Hetty hadn't lost her knack for taking the wind out of a person's sails.

"Besides," continued Hetty, shoving the blue silk aside, "you don't need it."

"I told you so," whispered Mrs. Potts triumphantly to Mrs. Bugle.

"And remember," continued Hetty, "we've come to shop for Sara, not for you. The child hasn't a thing that fits, and I do not have the entire day to fritter away on nonsense."

"That's true," Olivia said quietly. "Sorry to have troubled you, Mrs. Lawson."

"Pshaw. No bother, that's what I'm here for, Olivia!" replied Elvira Lawson, who was accustomed to Hetty running roughshod over the members of her family. Elvira began folding the blue silk and turned her attention to Sara. "You are getting tall, Sara Stanley," she said, admiringly. "I was noticing as you walked in. I said to myself, Elvira, they certainly grow them like weeds these days!" She laughed amiably and placed the blue silk back on the shelf. "So, a new dress, is it?" and she grinned at Sara. "Well, I know just the one, don't I?"

With that, Mrs. Lawson reached for the rose-colored crêpe-de-chine in the window. "All the girls just ooohh and aahh over this. It's a copy of a Paris original." She fluffed out the ruffles and bows for Sara to admire.

She needn't have bothered; Sara was already enraptured. "Paris!" she breathed. "I knew it, Mrs. Lawson! Probably from the Rue de Faubourg."

"That is precisely where they should have left it," snipped Hetty, eyeing the dress disdainfully.

Mrs. Potts and Mrs. Bugle, who had been preparing to leave, stopped dead in their tracks and hid behind the dressmaker's dummy. If there was one thing the good ladies relished, it was witnessing a family squabble first hand. Wouldn't this make a story to tell the ladies of the sewing circle!

"I bought all my clothes on the Rue de Faubourg when Papa took me abroad," Sara confided to Mrs. Lawson. "I think it's wonderful you're carrying dresses from France. Isn't it simply exquisite, Aunt Olivia?"

"More than exquisite. It's perfect!" replied Olivia.

"Perfectly awful," interjected Hetty, unwilling to lose a golden opportunity for a dig at Blair Stanley. "Your father didn't have the sense God gave geese, dragging a child halfway around the world to buy frills and frippery! Show me something sensible, Elvira."

"But I don't want something sensible," wailed Sara, "I want that dress. I love it!"

Mrs. Lawson reluctantly hung the rose dress back in the window and took a plain brown pinafore from the shelf.

"Well...there's this, Hetty," said Mrs. Lawson. "It's very practical, of course, but I don't think..."

"That's more like it," said Hetty approvingly as she fingered the rough brown material. "This'll wear like iron. I'll take it."

Sara stared at the pinafore, horrified. Not only was it babyish and ugly, but she could tell at a glance that it would scratch. She reached out and felt the cloth. Sure enough, bits of serge prickled her fingers. "It's horrible," she said. "I won't wear it!"

"Oh yes, you will," stated Hetty flatly, the matter finished. "Wrap it up, Elvira."

Mrs. Lawson looked weakly at Sara and began wrapping the pinafore. Olivia whispered gently to her sister, "Please Hetty. Be reasonable. If she won't wear it, what's the sense of buying it?"

"She'll wear it," Hetty declared, "and like it. I wore pinafores when I was young and what was good enough for me is good enough for Sara."

Olivia drew Hetty aside, hoping some gentle persuasion might do the trick. "Hetty dear," she said quietly, "what was in style then isn't in style now. Besides, Sara is growing up, she knows what she likes…"

"Sara is my responsibility," hissed Hetty, "and she will do as she's told!"

"Don't I have a say?" Sara broke in, insulted at being left out of such an important decision.

"No, you do not. Not with the price of clothes these days." Ignoring Sara completely, Hetty eyed the brown pinafore with satisfaction. "It's got a good big hem, it'll last you for years." She glanced down at Sara, certain the child would be persuaded by the logic of a sizable hem. "Wrap it up, Elvira."

"*Don't you dare wrap it up, Mrs. Lawson.*" Sara's voice had an icy edge of determination, and even Hetty was shocked. "I have my own birthday money from Nanny Louisa, so I'll take the Paris dress and pay for it myself."

"Good Lord," whispered Mrs. Potts to Mrs. Bugle, "I think Hetty King is going to blow a gasket."

Mrs. Lawson's eyes widened as Sara pulled the dollar bills from her purse. In Mrs. Lawson's years in business, she had learned one thing: he who pays the piper calls the tune. Hastily, she unwrapped the pinafore and reached for the rose-colored gown. But Hetty's cold stare stopped her dead in her tracks. Mrs. Lawson hesitated, holding the rose crêpe-de-chine in one hand, the pinafore in the other, suddenly unsure which piper was paying for what tune.

"*The pinafore, Elvira. I said wrap it up.*" Hetty's gaze was cold as ice, her own pocket-book open, money in her hand. Mrs. Lawson knew that those who tried to cross Hetty King always lived to regret it. So, with a sympathetic glance towards Sara, she reluctantly put the rose dress back in the window and began wrapping the pinafore once again.

"Really," continued Hetty, with a last, scornful glance at the Paris creation, "you'd best think twice before bringing such bilious confections into Avonlea and turning the heads of little girls like our Sara."

Little girls! Well, Aunt Hetty might think she could go on treating her like an infant, but Sara had no intention of letting her get away with it. Her gaze fell on a tempting display of chocolates. "How much are those, Mrs. Lawson?" she asked abruptly.

"Penny a bag, dear."

Sara rummaged in her purse. "I'll take a bag."

"You will not," declared Hetty. "You'll spoil your supper."

Again, Mrs. Lawson looked from one to the other, unsure what to do. This time, Sara didn't give her a chance to decide. With a stubborn glance at Aunt Hetty, Sara blurted out in a fury, "I will have chocolates if I want them! I am not a two-year-old!"

With that, she plunked her money down on the counter and, grabbing five chocolates in her fist, defiantly stuffed the lot of them in her mouth. Half choking, cheeks bulging, she raced from the store. The doorbell jangled; the door slammed.

Mrs. Potts and Mrs. Bugle almost keeled over from excitement. Olivia stifled a gasp and ran after Sara, causing the bells to jangle once again. Horrified, Hetty threw her money at Mrs. Lawson, grabbed the parcel containing the pinafore and sailed out the door in hot pursuit.

The bells jangled one last time and the door

slammed shut. Mrs. Lawson stared. At last, scooping up the money, she shook her head in confusion. "Good grief," she muttered to Mrs. Potts and Mrs. Bugle, who had emerged from behind the dressmaker's dummy, "what a tempest in a teapot!"

Chapter Three

Half blinded by tears, Sara raced down the road away from the general store, wiping her wet cheeks with a grimy, chocolate-covered hand and streaking her face in the process. She could hear Aunt Olivia behind her, calling frantically, "Sara! Wait for me!" Ruefully, she paused to let Olivia catch up.

Olivia looked at her bleakly. "Sara," she puffed, out of breath, offering her handkerchief, "for heaven's sake! Here. Use this." Sara took the handkerchief but mostly succeeded in smearing the chocolate even more. "Sara dear," Olivia chided gently, "you know you're not going to get anywhere with Hetty by deliberately crossing her."

"Don't care," mumbled Sara, taking a swipe at her tears with the lacy linen. It came away smeared with chocolate stains. "Now look what I've done, I've ruined your handkerchief. I'm sorry, Aunt Olivia, I can't do anything right anymore!"

Olivia knew how Sara felt. After all, as the youngest of Hetty's sisters, she had been in Sara's shoes once and knew what it was like living under Hetty's thumb. Still, if there was to be peace in the family, Sara must learn to deal with Hetty, and now was as good a time as any to start.

"Look, Sara, Hetty isn't peaches and cream, I'm the first to admit it. But you have to learn to be...diplomatic. You can't run off and do anything your—"

She stopped short. Hetty was rounding the corner and descending upon them, clutching her hat to her head and brandishing her parcel like a tomahawk.

"Sara Stanley!" piped Hetty, gasping for breath, her eyes bright with fury. "How dare you humiliate me in there...deliberately stuffing your mouth with chocolates after I told you no!"

Olivia put her arm protectively around Sara. "Let me," she whispered to Sara, who was only too happy to have Olivia's support. Taking a deep breath and facing Hetty squarely, Olivia intervened with what she imagined to be the utmost kindness.

"Hetty," she said, "please try to see this from both sides."

Hetty, with all the authority belonging to the eldest in the family, fixed her sister with a stare. "Stay out of it, Olivia."

"I can't," replied Olivia gently, "because this isn't entirely Sara's fault."

Now Hetty looked at her blankly. "I beg your pardon?" she said, in her most dignified schoolteacher's voice.

"You could have given her a choice. You didn't have to ram that pinafore down her throat."

Sara felt like cheering. She couldn't have put it better herself! Hetty, however, was vehement.

"I rammed nothing down anybody's throat, I did what was best for Sara by making a practical decision."

Sara looked quickly back at Olivia.

"Maybe," said Olivia, "but Sara is getting old enough to make certain decisions on her own."

Sara's heart soared. Yes! That was the point in a nutshell! Surely Aunt Hetty would see it and...

"Fiddlesticks," scoffed Hetty. "Until that girl shows some common sense, I'll make the decisions in this family, thank you very much! Come along, Sara, I have a bone to pick with you." With that she swept ahead, pulling Sara along with her.

Olivia wasn't about to let it go at that. She raced in front and blocked Hetty's path. "Honestly, Hetty," she said, exasperated, "I wish you would listen to someone's voice besides your own."

"Oh really?" snapped Hetty. "I see. Now my judgment isn't good enough, eh? I suppose you've forgotten everything I used to do for you? Who looked after you before you became Mrs. Jasper Dale? Who cared for you? Tell me, who?"

Olivia sighed. "You did, Hetty. And you'll never let me forget it." She looked sadly at

Sara. No matter what, Hetty always came out the winner in these discussions. How could she give Sara advice when she herself couldn't deal with Hetty without getting riled up? It was hopeless!

The rumble of wagon wheels approaching stopped Olivia from saying exactly that. She looked up to see Felix driving the rickety old buckboard, which was groaning under the weight of bushels of apples.

"Hello there!" Felix called out, pulling the horse to a halt, unaware that he was interrupting a family squabble. "Want to come over to our place, Sara?"

"She does not," sniffed Aunt Hetty, "she has homework to do."

"I'll do it later," muttered Sara, making a mad dash for the wagon and climbing aboard. "Hurry. Let's go," she whispered fiercely to Felix.

"Get down here this instant, Sara Stanley!" demanded Aunt Hetty, amazed at the girl's boldness.

Felix looked from one to the other, bewildered, unsure whom to obey. Sara didn't wait for him to make up his mind. She grabbed the reins from his hands, and, ignoring Hetty's orders, she urged the horse on. The wagon rumbled down the road in a cloud of dust, leaving Aunt Hetty with her mouth hanging open.

"Did you see that? She deliberately disobeyed me!" Hetty gasped.

"Do you blame her?" mumbled Olivia under her breath. She cast Hetty an I-told-you-so glance. Hetty, however, refused to acknowledge her sister's accusing look. Nose in the air, she strode ahead, and Olivia hurried down the road after her.

As the wagon rolled along, Sara told her tale of woe to her puzzled cousin.

"A dress! All I wanted was one little dress. Really, Felix, was that so terrible?"

Felix considered this for a moment. Dresses were not high on his list of important matters, ranking far behind horses and food and money. Still, from his experience with two sisters, he knew girls had different priorities. "Well," he offered soberly, "that depends. I guess it *is* terrible if you're you-know-who."

"But I'm not you-know-who," retorted Sara, "I'm *me*, and she wants me to be like *her*!"

"That's impossible," said Felix. "Who could be like her? Who would want to?"

"Nobody," was Sara's glum reply.

"Father says the best way to deal with Aunt Hetty is to let her rant and rave—say yes to everything and then plain ignore her."

"How can I ignore her when I'm living with her?" lamented Sara. "I think she's getting worse. And she's just so mean and stubborn! Honestly, Felix, if I don't start sticking up for myself, I'll be under her thumb for the rest of my life."

They both contemplated this awful thought. Felix cast her a consoling look, but he could tell by the determined set of her chin that Sara was not to be consoled.

On her way to town later that afternoon, Olivia hurried along the red dirt road past Rose Cottage, head down, hoping against hope that Hetty wouldn't spot her and want to talk about Sara's behavior all over again. As luck would have it, Hetty chose that precise moment to open the window and shake out a dust cloth. Instantly her shrill voice rang out, "Yooo-hooo. Olivia, come in for a bit!"

Olivia stopped dead in her tracks. With a sigh, she turned and walked reluctantly back to the house. Like it or not, she was in for another lecture.

Sure enough, over tea in the kitchen, Hetty didn't waste a moment launching into her litany of complaints. "As you can see," she sniffed, raising her teacup to her lips and nodding towards a pile of ironing in the basket, "Sara has neglected her chores and left them for me to do. Off playing with Felix somewhere, I'll wager. I tell you, Olivia, that child is impossible!"

"Hetty…" Olivia paused to choose her words carefully, "I know raising a young girl isn't easy…"

"Easy!" barked Hetty, "I'd rather raise chickens than children."

"Still, there are two sides to every story."

"Not in my house there aren't. In this house there is only one side, and it's mine. Sara knows full well what the rules are and she had better obey them."

Try as she might to avoid an argument, Olivia knew it was going to be impossible. "I understand how you feel," she said, with the utmost caution, "but Sara is getting older and, really Hetty, you still treat her like she's a little child."

"She acts like one," sniffed Hetty. "She doesn't have enough sense to fill a thimble."

"Well, maybe if you treated her a bit more like an adult, allowed her a little more independence, she'd behave differently." Olivia was close to losing her temper, in spite of her best efforts to stay calm.

"Really? I suppose since you became Mrs. Jasper Dale you're suddenly an expert on everything! Well, you're wrong." Hetty's face flushed deeply. "No," she said emphatically, "if I have erred at all, I fear it's on the side of leniency."

"Leniency! Good grief, Hetty King, you're about as lenient as a...a..."—Olivia struggled for the right words—"...as a brick wall in a windstorm! You never give in to anybody but yourself!"

Hetty's eyes widened and her teacup froze in midair as Olivia plunged on. "Don't you see? You're doing to Sara exactly what you tried to do to me! And it isn't going to work. She's going to grow up in spite of you...not because of you."

"Is that so! Well, I'll have you know Olivia Dale that I am—" Suddenly Hetty gasped, her voice coming to a dead stop as she stared in disbelief towards the doorway. Olivia turned to look in the same direction and choked out a small, "Oh no!"

There was Sara, her chin lifted defiantly, posing like royalty in the forbidden rose-colored crêpe-de-chine from the Rue de Faubourg.

"Tea!" Sara said, sweeping regally into the room, trailing garlands of jewelled flowers and bows as she made a beeline for the teapot. "How lovely! I'm dying of thirst. It was awfully dusty on the ride over with Felix."

Olivia and Hetty watched in stunned silence as Sara helped herself to a cup of tea. For a moment Hetty was too astonished to speak, but when she managed to croak out a few words, her tone was dripping with menace.

"Sara Stanley, take off that ghastly dress this minute."

"I won't," said Sara, her voice almost as icy

as Hetty's. "I bought and paid for it with my own money." Then, ignoring Hetty, she paraded before an astounded Olivia. "Don't you adore this dress, Aunt Olivia? Isn't it the most exquisite thing you've ever seen? I'm going over to show Felicity right now!"

Olivia swallowed hard. What on earth had possessed the girl? Clutching at straws, Olivia opened her mouth to mumble something, anything, when Hetty pounced on Sara with a vengeance.

"You are not leaving this house in that bilious creation! Take it off. Upstairs!"

"You can't make me!" retorted Sara stubbornly, her blue eyes shooting sparks of defiance. "It's mine!"

"Upstairs! Not another word!" said Hetty in a fury, seizing Sara by the collar, spinning her around and steering her towards the stairs. "March." A clatter of boots was all they heard as Sara ran tearfully up the steps and across the landing.

Hetty turned back to Olivia, fuming. "There, you see? You see how the child disobeyed me?" she sputtered, every bit as angry with Olivia as

she was with Sara. "It's all your fault, Olivia
Dale. So much for your foolish ideas about children and independence."

Olivia sat stock-still, heartsick at this turn of
events. Sara had done wrong, no two ways
about it, but Hetty had brought it on herself.
They were both stubborn. Stubborn and proud
to boot, that was the crux of the matter. She
sighed deeply, despairing of either of them backing down. From upstairs, as if underscoring her
thoughts, Sara's bedroom door slammed shut
with a harsh and bitter finality.

Chapter Four

Gus Pike sat on the steps of the lighthouse
mending a fishing net. The lighthouse was
where Gus made his home. No doubt some
people in the village thought it was a lonely
way to live, but Gus never needed much company, as long as he had his fiddle.

As he was working he heard a cheerful
whistling drift his way, and he glanced up to
see a sailor approaching over the crest of the

hill, a knapsack tossed over his shoulder.

"Ahoy there, mate," called the sailor. "You Gus Pike?"

"That I am," said Gus. "An' who might you be?"

"Just come ashore from the Eliza B. Got a message for ya, lad. From the mainland."

Gus put down his fishing net. "That so? What's it about?"

"You got to go over to the mainland right quick," said the sailor, "on account'a Captain Ezekial Crane's in a bind."

"Captain Crane?" Gus sucked in his breath. "What kind of trouble? Who told you?"

"Don't rightly know the fella's name," said the sailor, tamping his pipe and lighting up. "Fella gave me two bits, he did, an' he said give the message to young Gus Pike over on the Island."

"But where'm I supposed to find him...this fella?"

"Twister Lane, near the wharf. You hunt for the sign of the Black Parrot." The sailor drew deeply on his pipe and slung his knapsack back over his shoulder, preparing to go.

"Hey…hold on. Didn't he tell ya nothin' else?"

"Not a word, lad. Not a word." With that, the sailor waved and set off back across the field, leaving Gus staring after him, worried sick for the safety of his old friend Captain Crane.

Mrs. Potts could hardly wait to relate the latest incident to the sewing circle gathered around the stove in the rear of the general store. "Well, ladies," she whispered confidentially, "don't let it go any further, but remember the ruckus over Sara's dress?"

"The one Hetty wouldn't let her have!" said Mrs. Rae, pausing mid-stitch in her embroidery, eagerly anticipating a fresh tidbit of gossip.

"It got worse," said Mrs. Potts, relishing her role as the bearer of bad tidings. "Now, as I said, don't let it go any further, but Hetty King is having an absolute conniption fit."

"What's new about that?" scoffed Mrs. Rae, hoping for something juicier. "Hetty King's always having fits."

"What's new is, Mrs. Lawson told me in confidence there was a terrible to-do because right after Hetty ordered her not to, Sara came back to the store and bought the dress herself. Elvira heard that Hetty hit the roof, but you can't tell a soul!" whispered Mrs. Potts.

"Well, it's no secret," said Mrs. Rae, lowering her voice. "Elvira Lawson told me, too, so why can't I tell anyone?"

"She told you?" Mrs. Potts was taken aback. "Well, don't tell her I told you she told me."

"For heaven's sake, if someone tells me something, I never tell anyone they told me if they told me not to tell, you know that!" said Mrs. Rae huffily. "Anyhow, I feel sorry for poor Sara Stanley. Hetty's such an old pricklepuss."

"Young girls have their own ideas these days," added Mrs. Potts. "That's an awful big pill for Hetty King to swallow."

"Ha!" said Mrs. Bugle, jabbing a needle into her quilt. "It's high time somebody stood up to Hetty King. If you ask me, Sara Stanley's got spunk!"

In the kitchen of Rose Cottage, Sara stood at a sink full of dirty dishes, scouring a pot while Hetty circled around her like a buzzard.

"Use elbow grease, girl. How many times do I have to say the same thing? I swear it goes in one ear and out the other!" Seizing the pot from Sara's soapy hands, Hetty held it up for inspection. "Aha! Look at this! A lump of soup stuck to the side. Do you think I would dare cook in a pot with old soup stuck to the side? What would people say? I'll tell you what they'd say, they'd say sloth, *neglect*...never eat at Rose Cottage because they cook in dirty pots! Do you care what people think? No, you don't. Do you care about my reputation in the community? No, you don't!" A knock on the door interrupted her tirade.

"I'll get it!" said Sara, leaping at a chance to escape.

"You will *not*, you'll stay right here and scour this saucepan till it shines," ordered Hetty on her way out of the kitchen.

Sara stood fuming at the sink until curiosity got the better of her. Then she tiptoed to the kitchen door and peeked around the corner. Hidden from view, she saw Hetty open the door.

Gus Pike stood there, cap in hand, his face pale with worry.

"Miss King," he asked anxiously, "could I come in?"

"Why...what's the matter, boy? Of course you can come in."

Gus stood in the foyer, unsure how to start. He took a great breath and plunged right in. "Miss King, I gotta go to the mainland, it's real important."

Unseen in the shadow of the doorway, Sara was all ears.

"The mainland?" asked Hetty. "Is something wrong?"

"Yep. Seems like it. Captain Crane sent for me, and I gotta get there quick as I can." He hesitated, then cast an urgent look at Hetty. "Thing is, Miss King, I don't have the fare. But I got this..." He twisted a gold ring off his finger. "I'll give you my ring to hold if you could lend me the money. I'll pay you back, Miss King, honest." He held out the ring for her inspection. "It's real gold, Captain King gave it to me."

Hetty pushed the ring aside. "Pshaw. Never mind the ring. I'll help you, Gus Pike, of course I will." With that, she dug into her purse for some coins and pressed them into Gus's hand. "There you go, my boy."

"Thank you, Miss King...but I'd feel a whole lot better if ya took the ring..."

"Nonsense!" scoffed Hetty, "I trust you, Gus Pike. I know you're as good as your word."

From her hiding place, Sara listened, deeply hurt and more than a little envious. Aunt Hetty treated her like such a baby, and yet she spoke to Gus Pike with such respect. It wasn't fair, not one bit fair!

"Sure 'preciate this, Miss King," murmured Gus. "You always been good to me."

Hetty waved him off. "Happy to do it. You take care, Gus Pike. I hope your friend's all right."

Gus plunked his hat back on his head and retreated out the door, smiling at Hetty. She turned to find an incensed Sara looking at her, soapy hands on her hips.

"Why is it," Sara declared accusingly, "that Gus gets to do whatever he wants?"

Hetty looked down her nose at Sara. "Because he is a responsible person, that's why. Oh, he has come a long way, that boy, he knows how to take care of himself." Hetty smiled with satisfaction, recalling the days when Gus Pike hungered so to read and write that he would race to school exhausted after the early shift at the cannery and practically fall asleep at his desk by four o'clock. *That* was spirit! *That* was dedication to learning! *That* was the sort of person Hetty King admired!

Hetty drew herself up to her full height and ushered her indignant young charge into the kitchen. "Enough dilly-dallying, Sara Stanley. Back to the sink...and mark my words, if there's one dirty pot left, you'll hear about it."

Chapter Five

Sara perched on the steps leading up to the lighthouse, watching Gus Pike pack up some of his meager belongings for his trip to the mainland. Felix and Felicity had brought chicken sandwiches and raisin-drop cookies for the journey; Gus eyed these delectable treats and sneaked half a sandwich from its wrapping, chomping it down in a few fast gulps. Then he tucked the remainder into the bottom of the rucksack and flashed Felicity a grateful smile.

"Thanks a heap, Felicity, these'll sure come in handy."

"Not if you eat them before you get there," teased Felix. Felicity and Gus burst into laughter, but Sara remained silent, lost in her own glum thoughts.

"Hey, Sara…what's wrong?" asked Gus, knotting a rope around the torn rucksack.

Sara heaved a great sigh and, wagging a grim finger at Gus, launched into a perfect imitation of Aunt Hetty. "Good Lord, girl, you didn't scour the soup pot! Don't you know you can get bubonic plague from a dirty pot? What will the ladies at the sewing circle say? Where were you brought up, in a pigsty?"

The others stifled a smile and looked at one another knowingly, well aware of Sara's problem with Hetty.

"Honestly," Sara continued bleakly, "what's a person to do when the other person criticizes every single thing you say?"

"Maybe you're taking things too seriously," said Felicity, with a superior smile.

"Seriously?" Sara scoffed. How could Felicity understand her feelings? Nobody ever criticized *her*—except maybe Felix, and little brothers didn't count. "How would you like to be nagged and hounded and forced to wear clothes you hate?" Sara asked, offended all over again. Once more she adopted Hetty's prim voice and manner. "This ugly little pinafore has a good big hem and it will last you for years—you can wear it to college, you can be married in it and then you can be buried in it!"

This time the others roared with laughter. "Aw, Sara, your Aunt Hetty ain't so bad," offered Gus by way of comfort.

"No?" wailed Sara. "Then you go live with her."

"Hetty King's a tough old bird, but her heart's in the right place," Gus replied thoughtfully. Then he brightened, a solution to Sara's problem beginning to dawn on him. "I know!" he said, a grin crossing his face. "I betch'a if ya did somethin' she didn't expect... somethin' real grown-up-like, she'd be pleased as punch an' forgive ya for everything. Go on," urged Gus, sensing Sara's reluctance, "think o' somethin'. It can't hurt. Give it a try."

Hetty King bustled around her kitchen, oblivious to the fact that Felix and Sara were standing in the doorway. Sara was nervous and hopeful, waiting for the perfect moment to spring her surprise. Unable to conceal her excitement a moment longer, she cleared her throat and plunged ahead as Hetty hung the kitchen towel to dry.

"Aunt Hetty," she announced, "I have a wonderful idea."

Hetty raised an eyebrow. "Really? I can't fathom what that would be."

"It's very responsible."

"Ha," was Hetty's derisive reply. "*You* responsible? That will be the frosty Friday."

Undaunted, Sara forged on. "I think you'll be surprised," she said with confidence. "I've decided to take the dress back to Lawson's and put the money in my savings account."

Hetty smiled appreciatively at her niece. "That is commendable, Sara," she said, busying herself filling the salt shaker, "but I'm afraid you're too late."

"Too late...?" said Sara. The strangest feeling was brewing in the pit of her stomach.

"Yes," said Hetty, reaching now for the pepper, "I've already donated that dress to the Foreign Missions box at the church."

Sara's jaw dropped. "You did *what*?"

Hetty continued filling the pepper mill, sweeping specks off the table and into her cupped hand, then stifling a loud *achoooo*. "You heard me," she said, dabbing her nose with a handkerchief. "You've got a lesson to learn, young lady, and charity is as good a place to start as any. Remember, it is more blessed to give than to receive."

"But that was *my* dress!" sputtered Sara, her shock turning to fury. "You had no right to give it away! Go give something of your *own* if you want to be blessed!" With that, she whirled around and fled the room.

"Sara Stanley! Don't you dare talk to me in that tone of voice or I'll wash your mouth out with soap!"

Sara, however, was already out the door and storming across the field, tears streaming down her face.

Felix hurried to catch up with Sara, who was striding ahead of him towards the little white church on the hill.

"The nerve!" she raged. "The absolute nerve! I mean, first she won't let me wear it, then she *gives* it away without even asking!"

"That was rotten of her," agreed Felix, although for the life of him he couldn't understand all this fuss over a dress. "I always ask before I do something rotten," he added by way of solace.

They were rounding the corner of the church when they suddenly found themselves in the path of a flying coat! It was being hurled from the Foreign Missions box. They stopped short, for a dishevelled young girl was bent over the box, flinging clothes every which way. She wore a ragged jacket and dirty, torn skirt; a rough brown hat was pulled down over her ears and blond, straggly hair poked out from beneath the hat. Over her shoulder was slung the beautiful rose-colored dress, and she was stuffing some of the other donations into her burlap sack. She straightened up slowly and glared at the two intruders.

"You got staring problems?" sneered the girl. "Well...do ya?"

They were too amazed to reply, partly because the girl spoke so rudely but mainly because her blond hair and blue eyes made her look startlingly like Sara.

"Well, I know it's not polite to stare, " stammered Felix, "but...you two...you look exactly alike!"

"Yeah?" said the girl, jamming the pink dress into her sack. "So what?"

"I only thought...that is..." Felix reddened, unsure how to react to the challenge.

Sara had no such trouble; why, this little hooligan was taking *her* dress, the one she had bought and paid for, the one Aunt Hetty had the nerve to give away without asking! Sara had just opened her mouth to say so when the girl pointed a grubby finger menacingly.

"An' keep your mitts off my stuff, 'cuz I got here first."

Sara gulped. This wasn't going to be easy. Who knew what this awful person might say or do if Sara demanded the dress back? After all, the Missions Box *was* public property, anybody could take its contents without asking for permission. She tried a more diplomatic tack.

"I was wondering," said Sara, smiling sweetly at the dirt-smudged face glaring at her, "that is…how would you like to trade dresses?"

"Sara's got lots more at home. Millions," said Felix, brightly.

The girl eyed Sara up and down. "Oh? You rich or somethin'?"

"Sara's filthy rich," said Felix.

"Felix!"

"Well, she is," boasted Felix, "she's an heiress, she's got piles of money."

"Don't tell people that!" said Sara, reddening at the mention of her inheritance. The girl looked at Sara with increasing interest.

"If I was rich, I'd sure brag about it," said Felix.

"Tough life, eh?" the girl commented dryly, casting Sara a disparaging glance.

"Look here," said Sara, hurriedly putting diplomacy aside, "that was my dress. My aunt put it in the Missions Box by mistake and I came here to get it back."

"Suck my elbow," the girl retorted. "Why don't you shove off."

Sara realized she was up against an opponent who was not likely to hand over the dress without a fight, and from the looks of her, she'd win a fistfight hands down. She glanced hastily at Felix, but he was keeping his distance—he clearly had no desire to tangle with this wildcat! With a sinking heart, Sara decided it was prudent to give up and declare herself the loser.

"Come on, Felix," she said. "It's no use."

With a reluctant look at the girl, Sara prepared to retreat with as much grace as she could muster. "If you change your mind about that dress," she offered delicately, "please don't hesitate to come and see me. I live over at Rose Cottage."

Except for a sneering "La-di-da!" the girl didn't bother to dignify Sara's offer with a reply. Shouldering the sack, she tugged the hat down over her ears and swaggered off without looking back. Felix stumbled after her.

"Hey!" he shouted. "You never even told us your name."

She hesitated, then glanced back. "Jo Pitts," she tossed off loftily, "and I'll thank ya to shut yer big fat yap."

Sara sucked in her breath, appalled. What a strange person, she thought. Not a shred of manners! She was sure that Jo Pitts never worried about what other people wanted her to do. Still, you could never tell, she might have a change of heart about the dress.

"I meant what I said, Jo Pitts!" Sara called after her hopefully. "Come and see me. Rose Cottage is on the other side of the village just past the schoolhouse!"

Jo Pitts ignored her and kept on walking, free as a bird, until she'd disappeared into the woods.

Aunt Hetty won, thought Sara. With a sinking heart, she knew she would never lay eyes on that exquisite dress again.

Hetty's fingers drummed the kitchen table. The dinner table was fully set, the clock ticking well past the dinner hour, and Sara was nowhere to be seen. This was the last straw! Sara had already shown herself to be disrespectful and disobedient, and now she was adding tardiness to her list of crimes. Hetty decided that Sara must be taught a lesson, once and for all.

Sara chose that unfortunate moment to burst in the door, flushed and out of breath.

"Sara Stanley! You are over one hour late!"

"I am sorry, Aunt Hetty," she exclaimed. She hadn't meant to be late, she had just been so wrapped up in her thoughts about Jo Pitts that she had completely forgotten the time. "You see, I met this girl who—"

Hetty cut her off sharply. "Here I stand over a hot stove cooking a good meal for you and you're off Lord knows where. Don't you care that I'm waiting? Don't you care if I'm here eating dinner all by myself? I suppose you preferred Olivia's cooking, eh? Is that it?" She rode roughshod over Sara's attempt at an explanation, announcing curtly, "There's no hot supper for you now. I've put it away."

"I said I was sorry, Aunt Hetty," insisted Sara. "If you would only listen for two minutes—"

"Don't you give me any backtalk!" replied Hetty, sharply. "Sit down."

Hetty reached into the larder and retrieved a plate covered with a napkin. She plunked it down in front of Sara. "There. You'll have to eat your supper cold."

Sara lifted the napkin to find cold liver, brussel sprouts and a congealed glob of squash— food she disliked even when it was piping hot. Resolutely, she dropped the napkin back over it. "I'm not hungry," she said, rising from the table.

Hetty whipped the napkin off and pushed Sara back into the chair. "You are so. You're not getting up from this table until you've finished it."

"I said I am not hungry." Sara folded her arms stubbornly and glared at the wall.

Hetty, however, was not about to lose this fight. She shoved the plate closer to Sara. "*I said finish it.*"

"Fine," said Sara, slowly and deliberately dumping the plate onto the floor. "It's finished."

If it were physically possible for steam to shoot from Hetty's ears, it would have happened then and there. She was furious, and her face had turned beet red. "Why, you little *devil!*" she hissed, *"you clean that up!"*

Sara looked up at her aunt coolly. "Aunt Hetty," she said, "you tell me what to wear, you tell me what to eat, you tell me what to think. You don't respect me, so why on earth should I respect you?" Sara pushed the chair back from the table. She stood up. Then she pointed to the mess on the floor and said, *"Clean it up yourself!"*

With that, Sara fled the house, slamming the door hard behind her.

Hetty stood frozen to the spot, shocked silly. For a horrible moment, she stared at the mess on the floor. Never in all her born days had anyone defied her so boldly, so deliberately... so *outrageously!* Blood pounded in her head, and if she suffered a stroke and dropped on the spot it would all be Sara's fault! Oh, no doubt about it, the battle lines were drawn. If Sara Stanley wanted war, then war she would get!

Janet King couldn't believe her ears. Her niece, Sara? Polite, soft-spoken Sara Stanley confined to her room?

"It's true, Mother," Felix insisted. "Aunt Hetty said she's only allowed out to go to school."

"School and the outhouse," said Felicity loftily, relishing the fact that her cousin was out of favor.

"She'll be stuck in her room forever!" said Felix, enjoying the melodrama of his cousin's plight.

"Nonsense," said Janet, her mouth full of clothespins as she hung up laundry. "Don't exaggerate. You know what your father says, Aunt Hetty's bark is worse than her bite. She'll get over it. She always does."

"We have to do something, Felicity! Maybe we can visit her, use our geography test as an excuse…"

"With Aunt Hetty on the warpath?" scoffed Felicity. "Not me. I'm not getting into trouble."

"And you'll keep your nose out of it too, Felix King, or you'll end up in the same fix as Sara," warned Janet.

Felix nodded innocently, but he crossed his fingers behind his back, knowing full well he couldn't keep his nose out of anything for long.

Chapter Six

That very afternoon found Felix and Sara poring over an atlas, studying the continents, all the while keeping a watchful eye on Hetty, who was pinning on her hat, preparing to leave.

"North America, South America, Australia, Europe..." murmured Sara dutifully.

Hetty nodded her approval. Perhaps temporary house arrest was exactly what Sara needed to bring her to her senses, and a little extra study time would certainly improve her schoolwork. With a last glance to make sure all was well, Hetty slipped her coat on and headed for the door. "I'm off to pick up the mail, children. Be sure and behave yourselves."

"Yes, Aunt Hetty," said Sara obediently.

With a *humph!* and a *sniff*, Hetty was gone. The moment the door clicked shut, the children shoved the atlas aside and breathed a sigh of relief.

"Thank goodness," crowed Felix. "Let's have some apple pie!" The two of them hurried off to the kitchen.

They might not have dug into that pie with

such enthusiasm if they had happened to glance outside. There, in the garden, was a most unlikely sight: Jo Pitts was hopping over the picket fence and creeping furtively towards the clothesline. Her brown hat was pulled low around her ears, and she was wearing the rose crêpe-de-chine dress, which was somewhat the worse for wear, smudged with dirt and ripped in one or two places.

At that very moment, as Sara and Felix were helping themselves to pie and pouring glasses of cold, frothy milk, Jo Pitts was examining the blouses flapping wetly in the breeze. When a puffed-sleeved shirtwaist of Sara's caught her eye, she whipped it off the clothesline, hiked up her skirt and stuffed it deep into a pocket in her petticoat. Then, pleased with her haul, she prowled around the house, peering in windows, looking for treasure. And that was when she glanced inside the open parlor window and spotted Aunt Hetty's tea service gleaming on the sideboard. Without a moment's hesitation, she climbed in the window.

It was Sara who heard the strange *clunk-clunk* sounds coming from the parlor. She and

Felix tiptoed towards the door and peeked in. Stunned, they saw Jo Pitts reaching with one grimy hand for the silver teapot.

"Jo Pitts!" Sara exclaimed, shocked to see her in the house. "What are you doing here?"

The hand whipped away from the teapot as if struck by lightning. "Aw, nothin'," said Jo, smoothing down the folds of the pink dress over the lumps and bumps in the petticoat. "Just passing. I come to trade the dress like ya asked. The window was open so I come in."

Sara was about to advise her that most visitors use the door, not the window, when Jo reached for an apple from a bowl of wax fruit and bit into it with gusto. "Yech!" She gagged and instantly spit it out. "This is bloody awful!"

Sara stifled a giggle but Felix couldn't hold back his laughter. "It's wax," Sara said as kindly as she could. "Aunt Hetty keeps wax fruit in that bowl for show."

"Now ya tell me," said Jo, picking hunks of wax from between her teeth. Dubiously, she eyed the silver tea service. "What about that? Is that fake, too?"

"Oh no," laughed Sara, "that's sterling silver. It belonged to Grandmother King."

"Nice," murmured Jo, her eyes widening. She flashed Sara and Felix a crafty grin. "Granny King leave ya anything else?"

"Lots of things," replied Sara, confused by Jo's sudden interest in Grandmother King.

Jo Pitts was certainly a strange individual, thought Sara, and she decided it might be wise to resolve the matter of the pink crêpe-de-chine before she disappeared again. "If you like," Sara offered, trying not to appear too eager, "we can go upstairs and you can choose a different dress…"

"Yeah. Don't mind if I do," was Jo's reply. She lobbed the ruined wax apple towards Aunt Hetty's favorite velvet chair, where it bounced and rolled under a table. Then she marched towards the stairs as though she owned the place. Hastily, Sara retrieved the apple and placed it back in the bowl, teeth marks down so Aunt Hetty wouldn't notice the chunk missing.

"Whatch'a waitin' for?" said Jo impatiently, already halfway up the stairs. Felix and Sara exchanged glances, then they clambered up the stairs after her.

In no time flat, Sara's room looked like a cyclone had hit it. Dresses flew out of the cupboard, landing on the bed, the floor and the dressing table, as Jo rifled through the cupboard like a whirling dervish. Choosing a blue flowered smock, she ducked behind the door and changed, flinging the pink silk on top of the pile on the floor. Then she made a flying leap for the bed, landing in a tumble beside a wide-eyed Sara.

"Nice place you got here," she said, bouncing blithely on the feather bed. "You got this whole room to yourself?"

"Yes," said Sara. "This used to be my mother's room."

Jo was barely listening as she eyed all the treasures on Sara's dressing table...the gold rings and pins lined up neatly in a flowered china tray, the silver comb and brush, the tiny filigreed perfume bottles.

"All that stuff yours, too?" asked Jo, leaping off the bed to admire a delicate cameo pin.

Sara and Felix were watching her, so with great reluctance she put the pin back. Slapping Sara's straw boater on her head, she pirouetted before the mirror.

Sara felt Jo's envy keenly. She reddened, embarrassed to have so many worldly goods when Jo obviously had so little.

Felix, however, was looking at Jo as she paraded in front of the mirror in Sara's finery. "I can't believe how much you two look like sisters!" he remarked.

"Really?" said Sara, taking a long look at Jo herself. "You think so?"

All at once, they heard the door slam below and Felicity's voice calling out. "Felix…? Sara…? Are you up there?"

An impish grin lit up Felix's face. "Jo, you go down!" he whispered impulsively. "It's my nosy sister, see if you can fool her into thinking you're Sara."

"Don't be silly, Felix," hissed Sara. "Felicity's smart, she'll guess right off!"

"Betch'a she won't," said Jo, her eyes gleaming.

Sara stared at Jo. They *did* look alike…and it

would be such a lark to pull the wool over Felicity's eyes for once!

"Sara, I know you're feeling blue," called out Felicity. "That's why I came over. To offer you some advice about Aunt Hetty."

Sara and Felix stifled their laughter. Jo grabbed the cameo pin. "Betch'a this here pin I can do it," she said with a wicked smile.

"Come on, Sara, let's," urged Felix. "You've got lots of pins."

"Well…" said Sara, caught up now in the excitement of the adventure, "all right. But your face is dirty, we'll have to clean you up and brush your hair first!"

"Forget that stuff!" prodded Felix. "Just go! Hurry, before she comes up here!"

Sara quickly rearranged Jo's hat and tried to smooth her tangled hair, but Jo twisted away, wiping her nose with the back of her hand and smudging her already dirty face in the process. Then she clattered downstairs before Sara could make her picture perfect. Sara and Felix listened from the upstairs hallway, all the while fighting back gales of laughter.

Felicity smiled sweetly as Jo traipsed into

the room, but when she took a better look at the grimy face and tangle of hair, the smile faded from her lips. "Sara!" she breathed, appalled by her cousin's grooming. "What's happened to you?"

Jo marched past Felicity, heading straight for the cookies and stuffing a handful in her mouth.

"Sara Stanley!" called Felicity indignantly. "I'm talking to you."

"I heard ya," said Jo, heading for the parlor. Felicity stared at her and followed.

Upstairs, Sara and Felix convulsed with laughter as Felicity's voice floated up to them. "Just because Aunt Hetty took away all your privileges doesn't mean you have to be rude to *me!*" They giggled, picturing Felicity, hands on hips, trying to admonish Jo Pitts.

And in the parlor, Jo wandered about, carefully assessing any items that might be worth stealing. She ran her hands over the silver teapot.

"Really, Sara," said Felicity, "you look terrible. Awfully thin."

"All I get is bread 'n' water," Jo tossed off, coolly appraising a silver candy dish.

❧❧❧

"Oh, no 'ya don't," said Gus Pike firmly.
"You ain't running nowhere, I won't let you."
Sara stood her ground, her chin lifted stubbornly.
"You can't stop me Gus Pike. I'm going with you."

❧❧❧

"Sara Stanley, since you are so eager to participate
you'll say the continents at once!" demanded Hetty,
her voice rising. "The continents at once!" hollered
Jo Pitts, her voice rising to match Hetty's.

ஒஜஒ

"Pa! It's a trap. Run Sara, run!" shouted Gus Pike.
Abe Pike grabbed Gus by the neck, dragging him into
the shack and kicking the door shut in Sara's face.

❧❧❧

He lifted Sara off the ground and dangled her
like a fish on a hook.

"That's dreadful!" said Felicity, horrified. "Are you ill?"

"I'm terrible sick," muttered Jo.

"You *are?* What's the matter?" asked Felicity, all pity and compassion, her cousin's rudeness suddenly forgotten.

"Oh...sore throat. Fever." Jo clutched her throat to illustrate the pain she was suffering.

"Fever?" said Felicity, shocked.

"Got the shakes, too," said Jo, throwing a theatrical shiver into the bargain.

Felicity rushed to her side. "Oh, you poor dear!" She put her arms around Jo and hugged her, knocking off her hat.

A gold and ruby pin of Sara's tumbled out from under the hat and landed on the floor. Felicity stared at it. "What's that...?" she asked, reaching to pick it up.

Like a flash, Jo grabbed a thick handful of Felicity's hair and gave it a sharp yank. Felicity screamed and Jo Pitts scooped up the pin, jamming it back under her hat. "Keep your hands in yer pockets, ya filthy ol' witch!" snarled Jo.

"Sara Stanley!" gasped Felicity, stumbling

in fear for the door. She raced outside, fleeing for her life.

Jo stood in the doorway, yelling after her, "An' don't bother ever comin' back, ya hear me?" Satisfied, Jo dusted off her hands, slammed the door shut and ran back upstairs to announce to an astounded Sara and Felix that the hoax was a whopping success.

"You did it!" laughed Sara. "She thought you were me! Well, you certainly earned the pin, Jo Pitts!"

"Nothin' to it," boasted Jo, fastening the cameo to her flowered smock. "Easy as pie." She swaggered to the dressing table, where she admired herself in the mirror. "So," she said nonchalantly, "what else do you two do around here for fun?"

Chapter Seven

Hetty King marched along the red dirt road, brimming with self-righteousness and congratulating herself on her remarkable ability to handle difficult situations...difficult children in particular. She glanced at her watch. If she hurried, she could take a short cut across the field to the King farm and drop off their mail before returning home.

Oh, no doubt about it, she thought to herself as she raised her skirts just a snip above the ankle and picked her way through the tall, waving grasses, she understood children. After all, that was a schoolteacher's job, wasn't it? And, naturally, the child she knew best was Sara Stanley. Others might not agree with her methods—Olivia, for instance. But Olivia Dale's theories on child-rearing were nothing but hogwash—anyone with half a brain could see that! Why, it took years of experience to deal with a wilful girl like Sara Stanley, experience and wisdom and a good dose of common sense. Such traits apparently did not run in the family, for Olivia certainly displayed few of them. It was a good thing that she herself was Sara's guardian and the final authority where her welfare was concerned.

Yes, all things considered, Hetty felt in her heart that she had done the right thing by imposing strict discipline on Sara. The proof was in the pudding. Hadn't Sara come around? Hadn't she just left her studying geography at the kitchen table with her cousin, as calm and obedient a child as one could wish for? Yes indeed, the plan was working to perfection, and Hetty was delighted that she had stuck to her guns.

Just ahead was the King farm, where a row of freshly washed sheets snapped side by side in the breeze. Hetty's path was blocked by a low fence surrounding the property. Looking both ways to make sure no one would catch a glimpse of her ankles, she delicately hoisted her skirt, straddled the fence and hopped over.

All at once she caught the sound of voices, Janet's and Felicity's, coming from beyond the clothesline. They seemed to be disagreeing, and none too quietly. This gave Hetty pause, for if Janet could argue with a perfectly sensible child like Felicity, then Lord knows what the world was coming to. Hetty was about to barge into the conversation, but suddenly she heard her own name mentioned. She stopped dead in her tracks.

Now, if questioned, Hetty King would deny ever eavesdropping on anybody, but there she was, plain as day, straining to listen on the other side of a line of bedsheets. What she heard made her blood run cold.

"Oh, for heaven's sake, Felicity, don't be so ridiculous. Hetty would have told me if Sara was sick," said Janet. "I think she was just having some fun with you!"

"But I was just there!" said Felicity. "She looked terrible, and she told me she has a fever and the shakes, and I just know it's because she only gets bread and water to eat!"

Hetty's eyes widened and her hand flew to her mouth to cover a gasp.

"Hetty King would never starve a child!" Janet replied. "I say it's nonsense!"

This was the living end! Hetty whipped the sheet aside and turned to Janet.

"I don't call it nonsense," she hissed, her pinched face almost as white as the sheets flapping on the line. "Sara has lied. She told a bald-faced lie and she will answer for it!" With that, she stormed off again, leaving Janet and Felicity with their mouths hanging open.

"Hetty!" Janet called after her. "Wait! Don't jump to conclusions!" But her words were lost in the wind because Hetty was already halfway across the field, jumping to every conclusion imaginable.

"Who's the ol' battle-ax headin' this way?" asked Jo Pitts, glancing out the window of Sara's bedroom at the thin figure clutching her hat to her head and marching furiously across the grassy fields towards Rose Cottage.

Sara flew to the window. One look and she froze. "Oh no! It's Aunt Hetty! Quick, Jo—out the window!"

In a twinkling, Jo was shinnying down the tree, and before Hetty could reach the gate she had slipped away behind the house and was heading across the field towards the woods.

Felix and Sara sprang into action. They straightened the bedcovers and shoved the dresses underneath. When Hetty stomped up the stairs and burst into the room, she found the two of them studying the open atlas, just as quiet as church mice.

Hetty pointed a finger. "Felix," she ordered, her voice as cold as doom. "Go home."

Felix shivered. Without a word he dashed

out the door, clattered down the stairs and raced home to the King farm.

Hetty circled Sara, a hawk closing in on its prey. "Sara Stanley," she demanded, "what on earth did you tell Felicity?"

"Felicity?" said Sara innocently. "I didn't tell her anything."

"Oh yes, you did! I've been hearing stories. What's all this about bread and water? Why are you telling people that I'm starving you and making you ill? Come along, Sara, don't make things worse by telling me more lies!"

Sara had barely opened her mouth to protest when she caught sight of the rose-colored silk poking out from under the bed. Her heart sank. She tried to shove the dress back with her foot, but it was too late. Hetty's sharp eye had spotted it. If she was angry with Sara before, she was boiling now.

"Why, you deceitful, conniving little creature!" Hetty retrieved the dress from under the bed and waved it menacingly in Sara's face. "How dare you steal that dress out of the Missions Box after I expressly said you couldn't have it!"

"Aunt Hetty...I...I didn't steal anything!" sputtered Sara. "You don't understand—"

"I understand. I understand only too well. Your lies and disobedience were shameful, Sara Stanley. But now...now I find out you are a thief!"

"I'm not!" retorted Sara hotly.

"Don't lie to me, I will not tolerate lies! You are nothing but a bitter, bitter disappointment."

"I'm a disappointment?" Sara shot back defiantly. "You're nothing but a horrible old woman! You don't have one ounce of respect for my feelings!"

"Respect!" Hetty's voice rose a full octave. "What does respect have to do with it? You're a child—children respect adults, not the other way around!"

"I have feelings," Sara lashed out, her voice rising to match Hetty's, "but you wouldn't care about that because you're selfish and mean and you only care about *yourself!*"

"Selfish and mean am I? Well, thank the Lord your mother's not alive to see the way you turned out!"

Dead silence. Sara turned pale as a ghost. "My mother...!" she said in a whisper, deeply hurt, tears brimming. "If my mother were alive, she would love me no matter what!" Hot tears spilled over her cheeks. She bolted past Hetty, running pell-mell down the stairs.

Hetty stood stock-still.

"Sara...!" she called out, her heart pounding. "Sara..." But the front door slammed and she was left all alone, holding the offending pink dress in her hand, horrified by what her anger had caused her to say to the child she cared for so much.

Blinded by tears, Sara tore across the field to catch up with Felix, and between sobs she blurted out to him all the awful things that Hetty had said to her.

Felix knew there was little he could say by way of comfort, but at least he could lend her a handkerchief. "She didn't mean it, Sara," he said, "honest she didn't."

"She did so," sobbed Sara into the handkerchief. "I can't stand her another second."

"She'll get over it," said Felix, bleakly, "and

everything will get back to normal. Come on. Don't cry any more. Let's just go back to my house."

"No," blubbered Sara, "I don't want to go to your house, I don't want to go anywhere. I don't know what to do!"

"I know what *I'd* do," said a voice from out of nowhere.

They looked up sharply to see Jo Pitts, leaning against a tree, chewing on a long blade of grass. She sauntered over to Sara and glanced at her pityingly. "I'd just say, 'Kiss *that*, ya ol' battle-ax.' An' I'd take off."

"Take off?"

"Boom. Gone, that's how fast," said Jo, with a cunning smile.

"You don't mean...you'd run away?" said Sara, astonished, trying to conjure up Aunt Hetty's face if she ever did such a thing. She imagined Aunt Hetty furious, then forlorn... maybe even heartbroken. Then she thought better of it. Nothing would break Aunt Hetty's heart, it was made of stone.

"Yep. I'd run."

"Sara couldn't do that," said Felix firmly.

"Yeah? Why not? Who's gonna stop her?" sneered Jo.

"Why...Aunt Hetty, that's who," stammered Felix, shocked that Jo would make such a suggestion.

"She won't stop ya if she don't know you're gone," said Jo matter-of-factly, while digging dirt out from under her nails.

"What do you mean?" asked Sara. Aunt Hetty might have a heart of stone but she'd certainly notice if Sara were missing.

"Well..." said Jo, "I could live at Rose Cottage for a while. Fill in for ya."

Live at Rose Cottage? Jo Pitts? Maybe they hadn't heard her correctly.

"You'd pretend you were me?" asked Sara, eyes wide as saucers.

"Yep."

"Uh-oh." Felix was beginning to smell trouble. "I don't think that's such a good idea."

"Aw, shut your yap," said Jo scornfully, "you're catchin' flies."

Sara was quiet. You could almost hear the wheels turning in her brain. "You and me...we'd switch places."

"Sara!" said Felix, getting more and more worried by the minute.

Sara ignored him, her gaze fixed on Jo Pitts. Then she wiped away the last trace of a tear and a smile slowly lit up her face. "You know what, Jo Pitts, that is an exceptional idea!"

"No, it *isn't!*" yelped Felix, aghast. "You can't!"

"Why not? Jo fooled Felicity, didn't she? And besides, Felix, it isn't as though she'd do it all alone. You'd help her."

"Me?" It was one thing for Jo Pitts to make crazy suggestions, but why drag *him* into it? He was already feeling a noose tightening around his neck.

"Oh please, Felix, please say yes, it's really a perfect plan! I'm so tired of Aunt Hetty dictating to me and making me be somebody I'm not. Come on," she begged, "it'll only be for a couple of days. Besides, I'd love to see Aunt Hetty try to push Jo Pitts around!"

"No! Don't even think about it because it won't work…" Felix was desperately trying to squirm his way out of this mess.

"It *will* work!" said Sara, jumping at the challenge, more determined than ever. She looked Jo Pitts up and down, then said seriously, "But you'll have to learn my habits if you're going to trick Aunt Hetty."

"What kind'a habits?" asked Jo warily.

"Well...for instance, I brush my hair a hundred strokes every night."

"*A hundred strokes?*" scoffed Jo Pitts. "I'll go bald."

"No, you won't," Sara said. "Brushing makes your hair shiny." She eyed Jo and knew instantly that Aunt Hetty would throw a conniption fit when she saw that grimy face and those hands! A potato field of dirt was lodged under Jo's ragged nails. Sara hesitated. Would Jo bite her head off if she dared mention anything as delicate as bathing? She decided that forewarned is forearmed. "Aunt Hetty is very strict about cleanliness, Jo. You'll have to take a hot bath every night."

"Every night?" Jo was hard put to imagine getting soaking wet on purpose every single night. "Forget it," she said firmly, "I ain't doin' that."

"I think you'll have to," said Sara. "And you'll have to wear clean clothes every day."

Jo rolled her eyes in disgust. "With all that brushin' an' bathin' an' changin', no wonder you ain't got time for fun."

"Fun," said Sara, "is what I'm going to have when I leave."

"Leave!" gulped Felix. "You can't leave!"

"I can so!" retorted Sara. "Besides, you'll be here, you can coach her."

"Me?" Felix stared from one to the other in desperation. "You can't do this! Stop it, Sara, it's *dead wrong!*"

"It is not dead wrong and for once I will do as I please!" said Sara, fiercely stamping her foot. "In fact, Felix King, I am leaving right this minute." And with that she marched off, heading for the main road.

Felix stared at her, his mouth agape. Sara wouldn't *dare* run away and leave that awful Jo Pitts in her place. She *couldn't*. It was wild and foolish. Aunt Hetty would skin her alive! And when she found out that he had helped her...

"Sara, no!" he yelled. "Come back!"

But Sara was running even faster. She turned and waved at them, her chin lifted stubbornly.

"I'll come back. All in good time!" And she disappeared over the crest of a hill, flying like a bird that has just been released from its cage.

Felix cast a helpless look at Jo Pitts.

She shrugged at him, a nasty smirk on her face. "Hey," she said, slapping him on the back and almost knocking him over, "you an' me, we're gonna be pals, eh Felix?"

Pals with Jo Pitts? His heart sank like a stone. They were headed for disaster. His mother and father and Aunt Hetty were bound to find out, and they'd be sure to hold him responsible! He broke out in a cold sweat at the very thought.

"Oh sure," he groaned miserably, "we'll be pals."

Chapter Eight

Hetty King prided herself on her backbone, and her strength in the face of adversity. That was something the Kings were noted for. But most of all, she took secret pleasure in her ability to conceal her emotions, a talent that she employed every day of her life as a schoolteacher. Today, however, was different. Today, she hid nothing. Today, Hetty King was a nervous wreck.

She paced back and forth, shaken and guilty, pouring her heart out to Olivia, who was trying to paint the new dressing table Jasper had built for her.

"How could I have said something so terrible? How *could* I?" wailed Hetty.

Easy as pie, thought Olivia wryly. Saying terrible things was Hetty's specialty. But she always felt remorseful when she'd had a chance to calm down. With a sigh, Olivia wiped the brushes and put them to soak in a can of turpentine.

"You mustn't be too hard on yourself," Olivia said gently. "Everyone says things they regret."

"Not like this they don't," moaned Hetty, wringing her hands as she remembered the painful scene with Sara. "This was simply unforgivable."

Olivia sighed deeply. "Good Lord, Hetty, how on earth did the two of you ever get into such a pickle?"

"I don't know, truly I don't. One cross word led to another, I suppose." She cast a mournful glance at Olivia. "I should have kept my mouth shut."

"True," agreed Olivia, "but the thing is, you didn't. So you better go back there and tell her you're sorry. And I mean about everything."

Hetty stopped pacing. She stared at Olivia.

"Sorry...?" If there was one word that did not trip lightly off Hetty King's tongue, it was "sorry." She might wish she could stuff the awful things she uttered back in her mouth, but sorry...oh no, that wouldn't do. If you went about saying sorry to people, they would think you were lacking in conviction, they would take advantage, all sorts of terrible things might ensue. She looked ruefully at her sister.

Olivia, however, was determined to make Hetty face facts. "Now look," she said, "I warned you. Didn't I tell you that you were smothering her? That's not the way to treat a bright, high-spirited girl like Sara. Pull up your socks and let Sara have the last word for a change. And don't be such a stubborn mule. Give her a little freedom, for heaven's sake!"

"How dare you call me a mule! I didn't come here for criticism, I came for advice," said Hetty indignantly.

"And I'm giving it to you, if you'd only listen! Go home and do as I say, and you won't regret it!"

With an obstinate *humph!* and *sniff*, Hetty King glared at her sister, jammed on her hat, turned on her heel and sailed out the door.

Olivia sighed for the tenth time that afternoon. Convincing Hetty King to change her ways was like moving a mountain. On second thought, Olivia mused, moving a mountain might be easier.

As soon as Sara disappeared, Jo Pitts gleefully dashed over to Rose Cottage to take her place. Now she was bouncing around Sara's bedroom, snooping in drawers for treasure. She had just got her hands on a little wooden chest with a key in its lock when she heard the front door open and close. Deciding that she had better buy some time before confronting "the ol' battle-ax," she leaped into bed, pulled the covers up to her chin and pretended to be asleep.

Hetty ran up the stairs and paused outside Sara's door. She rapped lightly. "Sara...?" No answer. She hesitated, then turned the knob and entered.

Hetty's hand flew to her heart at the sight of the little blond girl sleeping so peacefully in bed. Why, she is just an innocent child, she thought with a sudden rush of emotion. How could I have been so hard on her? The very thought brought a lump to her throat. Could Olivia have been right about saying sorry?

Hetty agonized as she gazed tenderly at the sleeping girl. Then she squared her shoulders. Very well. If apologies were due, Hetty King would not shirk her duty. No indeed. When Sara wakened in the morning, Hetty would make amends and suggest they start afresh. A new dawn, a new day, she murmured happily.

Hetty tiptoed to the bed and ever so gently leaned over and gave the child a peck on the cheek. Luckily, she did not notice Jo Pitts screw up her nose and wince.

"Goodnight, Sara dear," murmured Hetty. "When you get up in the morning, I'll whip up a stack of buttermilk pancakes with strawberry preserves, just the way you like them." Brimming with goodwill, Hetty tiptoed out of the room and closed the door softly behind her.

Jo's eyes flew open. "Yech!" she muttered, wiping invisible traces of the kiss from her cheek. Then she leaped out of bed and made a dive for the little wooden chest. With a twist of the key, the lid clicked open to reveal a glittering array of bracelets, necklaces and pins. She chose one slim, engraved bracelet and bit it hard to make sure it was solid gold. Satisfied, she stuffed it into the pocket of her petticoat.

Downstairs she could hear Hetty rattling around the kitchen. Jo wished it were morning—she was starving! She bounced back onto the bed to examine the rest of the treasures. Things were looking up, all right, what with the old battle-ax cooking for her, a real feather bed to sleep on, clothes, Granny King's silver tea service ripe for the picking! What could be sweeter? She chortled with glee. One thing for sure, the ol' hag was going to be a pushover. Plucking Rose Cottage clean would be like taking candy from a baby!

Chapter Nine

The sun had barely risen in the pale dawn sky when Gus Pike picked up his rucksack and joined the travelers on the rickety old dock waiting to board the ship for the mainland. He was thinking about Captain Crane, and wondering why he'd been summoned so mysteriously. Was his old friend in some sort of trouble, and, if so, would he really be able to help?

Maybe because he was lost in thought, he didn't see the small, fair-haired girl who jumped off a farmer's wagon, thanked the farmer for the ride and then slipped quietly in line behind him. She waited until he was just about to board the ship, and then she caught his attention.

"Gus! Hello there!"

He looked up, startled. "Sara…?"

He was so astonished, she couldn't help but laugh. "It's me all right," she said, digging into her purse for money to purchase her ticket. "And just in time, too. I'm going to the mainland."

"You are? You never said you was goin' anywhere," said a puzzled Gus.

"Well," replied Sara, "I...I decided all of a sudden."

"Miss King never mentioned nothin' about it. Say...where is she?" asked Gus, looking around for Hetty as the line inched forward.

"Oh...she isn't coming." Sara bit her lip. She needed Gus's help if her plan was going to work.

"What do you mean she isn't coming...?" This was the moment she was dreading, because Gus Pike might be terribly angry and send her straight home. Still, she couldn't tell him a fib. "Aunt Hetty isn't coming," she blurted out in a rush, "she isn't coming because she's back at Rose Cottage and Gus, don't be angry until you hear me out, I'm running away because I'm sick and tired of the way Aunt Hetty treats me."

Gus stared at her, unable to believe his ears. "You're running away...?"

She nodded.

"Oh no, ya don't," he said firmly, "you ain't runnin' nowheres. I won't let you."

She stood her ground, her chin raised

stubbornly. "You can't stop me, Gus Pike. I'm going with you."

"You can't do that!" Now Gus was genuinely worried. "You gotta go home!"

Sara's blue eyes brimmed with tears. She looked earnestly up at him, knowing this was her one and only chance to convince him. He *had* to help her, he just *had* to. "Please, Gus Pike! You don't know how desperately unhappy I've been. If you make me go back, I'll just run away again, I swear I will." Tears were now running down her cheeks.

Gus flinched. The one thing that made him weak in the knees was seeing someone cry.

"I can't tolerate living with her anymore, Gus. I need to get away from her for a little while, that's all! If you take me with you I promise I'll be good as gold and I won't bother you in the least, cross my heart and hope to die."

Other passengers were milling around them in a crush to board. Sailors were sealing the hold and loosening the ship's mooring ropes in preparation. Gus was torn. He had important business on the mainland, and now here was Sara Stanley throwing a monkey wrench into things with her crocodile tears! Well, he couldn't leave her at port all alone, that was sure and certain, and he couldn't trust her to get home safely by herself, Hetty King would never forgive him if anything happened to her. Like it or not, he was forced to take her along. Drawing himself up to his full height, he laid down the law.

"Now, look here," he said sternly, in a tone that sounded disturbingly like Hetty King's. "Draggin' you along ain't what I planned but I got no way around it, so I guess I'm stuck."

"That means you'll take me?" cried Sara.

"Guess I have'ta. But here's the rules. You stick by me and do what I say, no wanderin' off, no monkey business, no talkin' back, no nothin'. That clear?"

"Oh, I promise! I won't get in your way at all. You'll see, I'll be a big help to you, Gus Pike. You won't be sorry!"

"Yeah, sure ya will," muttered Gus to himself, already regretting his decision. The ship's horn boomed across the water. "Come on, then," he said, reluctantly shepherding his young charge aboard.

Moments later the walkway was raised and the ship slipped away from its moorings. Sara's heart thudded with excitement as she stood at the railing, watching the Island slowly fade into the mist and disappear from view. She turned at last to gaze out to sea, her heart pounding. She had done it! A few heavenly days away from Aunt Hetty, and all it took was courage and the good fortune to meet up with Jo Pitts!

Cool ocean breezes ruffled her hair. The sea was so blue...a serene, steadfast blue, washing away all moods, all worries, yet holding forth the promise of strange and mysterious shores. She breathed deeply, delighted with herself and filled with the exhilarating spirit of adventure. The one fly in the ointment, of course, was Gus Pike. She stole a worried glance his way and saw that his usually cheerful face was looking rather glum as he gazed at a flock of gulls darting and swooping towards the water. He was none too happy with her at the moment. For a split second, she felt guilty because she had neglected to tell him about Jo Pitts. Then she shrugged it off. She would tell him later. Perhaps on the trip home when he would be in better humor.

She decided she was worrying for nothing and resolved to banish all dark thoughts from her mind. Jo Pitts might have a lot of faults but she was right about one thing: a person has to have fun once in a while, and if setting off on an adventure wasn't fun, what was? Besides, she assured herself as she lifted her face to the warmth of the sun, in a few days she'd be right back in boring old Avonlea doing the same boring old things and no one would be the wiser!

Chapter Ten

Jo Pitts yanked a pile of dresses from Sara's closet and chose a pretty smock with a lace collar. She held it against her body and studied the effect in the mirror. Eyeing her reflection, she stuck out her tongue, then flung the smock to the floor and carelessly kicked it aside, fancying another. She had dropped the second one and was reaching for a third when Hetty's voice rang out from downstairs.

"Sara! Breakfast's ready, dear."

Jo dug into the closet and yanked out a box of ribbons, choosing a bright-blue satin and dumping the rest on the floor. She tied the blue bow around her head, added a streamer of silk flowers and threw more dresses and shoes willy-nilly. Then she ripped open an embroidered case containing scarves and rifled through them, tossing them into the air like so much colorful confetti. A fancy embroidered shawl that Sara's father had once purchased for her in Spain caught Jo's eye. She wound it around her waist and waltzed about the room like a vain and spoiled contessa. As an added touch, she plucked a velvet cloak from the bottom of a pile of coats on the floor and draped it casually over one shoulder.

"Sara dear," trilled Aunt Hetty. "I'm waiting!"

Jo grimaced. "HOLD YER HORSES, YA OLD BAT!" she yelled, continuing to rummage through a clutch of beautiful Venetian glass beads, bedecking herself with a dozen or so strands of the exquisite necklaces.

At the foot of the stairs, Hetty bit her lip

and fell silent. "I know you're upset," she called out gingerly, desperately trying to be sweet, "but did you call me...an old...bat?"

Upstairs, Jo Pitts smirked into the mirror and called back innocently, "No, Aunt Hetty. I said 'Where's my *hat*?'" Then, doubling over with laughter, she added under her breath, "ya old bat."

Hetty had no idea what to make of this but decided it would be better to hold her tongue than to make the child unhappy again. Ever so gently she called out, "Better hurry, Sara dearest...we'll be late for school."

A moment later, Jo Pitts clattered down the stairs and into the kitchen. "Nice day if it don't rain," she muttered, pushing rudely past Hetty and plunking herself down at the table. She looked at the empty plate. "Hey. Ain't nothin' ready?" she demanded, fork in one fist, knife in the other.

Hetty's jaw dropped. It wasn't so much the grammar and the language—though that was bad enough—but really, the child looked a fright! Sara was always so meticulous, and here she was, her face streaked with dirt and her hair sticking out every which way. And why on earth was she dressed like a clown? Why, she looked positively garish wearing all those necklaces and bows and flowers at once. The colors! And that cloak! How could she even think of wearing that ridiculous velvet creation, slung over her shoulder as if she were off to the Paris Opera instead of school!

"Hey!" barked Jo. "Didn't ya hear me? I asked ya, ain't nothin' ready?"

It took every ounce of strength Hetty could muster to restrain herself. She took a big breath and said with a shaky voice, "Mind your grammar. Remember, we don't say 'ain't' in this house!" Then remembering her resolution to be lovable no matter what, she forced a weak smile and murmured, "Oh well, silly me, what's a little 'ain't' now and then."

Now, what to do about Sara's dreadful choice of clothing? Should she speak out, make an oh-so-discreet comment, and risk insulting the child all over again...or should she bite her tongue and let it pass? Another quick glance at the bows and flowers and Hetty decided silence was unendurable. It was her duty to say something.

With a smile, and trying not to offend, Hetty murmured nervously, "Play-acting, are we, dear? Dressing up a bit for a little joke? My, my, we certainly look...unique!"

"Thanks," muttered Jo. "Where's the eats?"

Hetty's heart sank. It seemed Sara was determined to go to school in this awful get-up. The old Hetty would have sent her directly upstairs to change. In the name of peace, however, the new Hetty was determined not to criticize or offend.

"Oh Sara," she said softly, "I don't blame you for being short with me, dear...considering the things I said to you yesterday."

"What things?" said Jo.

"It's sweet of you to pretend you've forgotten," cooed Hetty. "But my dear, I cannot forget."

"Forget what?" asked Jo, scratching her head with the fork.

Hetty winced but let it pass. "What I said to you, dear. Will you accept my most heartfelt apologies?"

Jo looked around the room, slightly confused. "You talkin' to *me?*"

"Oh yes!" said Hetty fervently. "To you, dear. I want to say from the bottom of my heart that I'm sorry."

Jo looked at her and shrugged. No skin off her back if the ol' bat wanted to babble on. She stretched out a grimy hand. "Suits me. Shake on it?"

Hetty stared, bewildered. Then she clutched the hand gratefully in hers. "Oh yes, yes…shake, of course!"

Jo shook her hand, then pumped it harder and harder, almost wrenching Hetty's arm from its socket. Determined not to protest, Hetty murmured an agonized, "Uh…Sara… that's enough, dear." But Jo was enjoying this no end and she gave Hetty's hand a yank that almost threw her over. Hetty grabbed the chair to steady herself and squeaked out a gentle, "There, now, Sara, that's fine, fine. I'll dish you out breakfast, dear."

Clutching her sore arm, Hetty limped to the stove and heaped a stack of pancakes on a platter, dabbing generous pats of butter on top and drizzling strawberry preserves over that.

This was Sara's favorite breakfast, certain to put her in a pleasant frame of mind. Her heart warming at the thought, Hetty stole a glance towards the table. There was Sara, dirty, dishevelled, looking like an absolute scarecrow, calmly picking her nose. For an awful moment, Hetty wanted to scream. But she restrained herself and rolled her eyes heavenward instead.

"Good Lord," she prayed under her breath, "I will never ask for anything again as long as I live. Just give me strength to get through this."

Chapter Eleven

Pale sunshine was showering through a fringe of spruces beyond the schoolhouse as the children played in the schoolyard, waiting for class to begin. With a scarf tied over her eyes, Cecily was playing blindman's buff. Josie spun her around until she was dizzy. Then she scrambled wildly, arms outstretched, while the others flew in all directions.

Felix looked as though he hadn't slept all night. As soon as he spotted Jo Pitts, he anxiously pulled her around the side of the schoolhouse. "Listen, Jo," he said earnestly, "Aunt Hetty knows that Sara and I worked really hard preparing for the geography test."

"Yeah?" snapped Jo. "So what?"

"So you better know your stuff as well as Sara did."

"Easy as pie," sneered Jo.

This didn't wash with Felix. "Look, I better practice the questions with you." He thought for a moment. "Where is Australia?"

"Don't you know?" asked Jo.

"Of course I know. I'm asking you," said Felix, testily. "Where is it?"

"Where's what?" said Jo.

"*Australia! Where's Australia!*" yelled Felix.

"How'm I supposed to know?" muttered Jo. "It's wherever you left it, I guess."

The jangle of the school bell cut the lesson short. Felix shot her a desperate glance. How could she be so stupid? Aunt Hetty would catch her out in no time flat!

"Come on," he said bleakly, "just keep your head down and your mouth shut or you'll get us both in *big* trouble."

She shrugged and tossed the velvet cape over her shoulder. With great trepidation, Felix led her into the schoolhouse.

Once inside, Jo Pitts looked idly around and plopped herself down in the last seat in the last row, as far removed from Hetty King as she could manage.

"Not there!" hissed Felix, pointing closer to the front. "Sara sits up there."

Jo swung over to the proper seat and Felix breathed a sigh of relief. So far so good. None of the other pupils seemed to notice anything wrong, and Aunt Hetty had only glanced briefly at Jo and had even smiled at her.

For the life of him, Felix couldn't understand how Aunt Hetty could put up with Jo Pitts, let alone allow her to come to school in that strange-looking outfit. He wondered if Jo was part gypsy. Maybe she had special powers and hypnotized people into doing whatever she wanted! The thought sent a shiver down his spine. Well, gypsy or not, he doubted if Jo

Pitts possessed magical powers that would help her pass a geography test!

"Good morning, class," said Hetty, rapping with her ruler on the desk for attention.

"Good morning, Miss King," chorused the class, minus one voice.

"Good mornin', Aunt Hetty," shouted Jo.

The rest of the class stared at Jo. Felix gulped. She was going to catch it now for sure! But Aunt Hetty only smiled, though rather tautly. Felix found this most curious. Aunt Hetty *had* to be hypnotized.

"I hope everyone prepared for the geography bee," said Hetty, surveying her pupils. "Now, who can tell me how many continents there are?"

"I can't," shouted Jo.

Felix groaned and shrank into his seat. Hetty clenched her fists and counted to ten. If her patience was to be tested, then she would stand up to the test, come what may.

"I did not ask you who *couldn't*, Sara Stanley," she said, gritting her teeth, "I asked who *could*. And you know very well we raise our hands when we have something to say."

Immediately both of Jo's hands shot up in the air, waving back and forth like windmills. Felix cast her a mortified glance and the other children tittered nervously, fully expecting Hetty to hit the roof.

"Stop it," whispered Felix, leaning towards Jo.

"Felix, mind your own business!" ordered Hetty, whacking the desk with her ruler. Felix jumped back, bewildered.

Hetty managed a smile at Jo, all the while wondering how much more she could tolerate of this ludicrous behavior. "Sara," she said, "since you are apparently so eager to participate, perhaps you'll begin by telling us the names of the continents."

Jo sat perfectly silent, looking at the ceiling, ignoring Hetty.

"Go on, up, up," prodded Hetty. "On your feet, girl. The continents."

Jo wriggled around in her seat. She scratched her head and glanced at Felix, but she kept her mouth shut. The class stared from Hetty to Jo and back again, waiting for the explosion that was sure to come.

"I am listening, Sara," said Hetty, color rising in a red wave from her neck to her face. A nervous edge crept into her voice. "Would you kindly name the continents, Sara."

Dead silence. Felix sank even lower in his seat.

Hetty's face was beet red now. "Sara Stanley," she demanded, her voice rising. "*Say the continents at once!*"

"*The continents at once!*" hollered Jo Pitts, her voice rising to match Hetty's.

The children burst into raucous laughter. Hetty hit the desk with her ruler. "No! No! No!" she yelled, "When I say to say the continents at once, I don't mean say 'the continents at once,' I mean say the continents *immediately!*"

"*The continents immediately*," yelled Jo Pitts.

Now the class roared, slamming their hands on their desks and cheering wildly. Felix groaned. Hetty thwacked her desk with her ruler, screaming at the top of her lungs, "Silence!! Silence!" But the class was out of control, laughing hysterically.

"Settle down now!" begged Hetty. "Children, settle down!"

Finally, there was nothing she could do but ring the bell for recess.

Felix couldn't wait to give Jo Pitts a piece of his mind. He dodged Aunt Hetty, who was standing white-faced and wild-eyed on the schoolhouse steps, and caught up with Jo. "Meet me behind the schoolhouse," he muttered, as fiercely as he could.

"Go stand on your head an' spit nickels," said Jo, thumbing her nose at him and refusing to budge.

"I have to talk to you, Jo Pitts!" he whispered, quickly glancing around to see who was listening. So far nobody was looking in their direction. "How could you act so stupid? I told you to keep your mouth shut. You really made a mess of things."

"Butt out, poophead," she sneered. A few heads turned, eyes widening in astonishment. "I'm the boss now." She grabbed Felix by the collar. Lowering her voice a notch, she warned, "You open your big fat yap an' I'm gonna tell the ol' battle-ax my takin' Sara's place was all your idea!"

"Shhhh!" begged Felix, casting a weak grin at Felicity, who was staring curiously at them from across the yard. "You can't tell, you can't!"

"Who says?" sneered Jo, and without a moment's hesitation, she hauled off and punched him squarely in the nose, sending him reeling backwards. Children gasped. Felicity screamed. Hetty ran towards them, arms waving wildly.

Felix lay on the ground, stunned, as blood spurted from his nose.

"Felix, Felix, speak to me!" said Hetty, kneeling over him and frantically wiping his bloody nose with her handkerchief.

Jo Pitts merely smiled. She dusted off her hands and strode off, innocent as an angel.

Chapter Twelve

Hetty marched across the lawn of the King farm, a plate of her very best raisin cookies in her hand as a peace offering. Janet would be furious, and she had every right to be. Bloodying anybody's nose was bad enough...but a *cousin's?* Sara's behavior was inexcusable, and as her guardian, Hetty had to take her share of the responsibility.

Hetty pursed her lips primly. She had tried her best with Sara, no one could have tried harder. She had resorted to kindness only as a last straw, and it hadn't worked. It would be a frosty Friday before Sara Stanley saw freedom again! But if the truth be told, Hetty King was stymied. She couldn't think of a single punishment that she hadn't already tried. Hetty King, who had devoted her entire adult life to the care and teaching of children and had never been known to fail at her task, had now failed with her own niece...and failed miserably.

She rounded the corner to the porch and saw Felix on the stoop, a big wad of cotton stuffed up his swollen nose. Janet was sitting next to him, feeding him applesauce and cream. Felix wanted to fade into the woodwork. Janet, however, smiled pleasantly at Hetty.

"Now Janet," Hetty said hastily, "I know we've had our differences, and I've certainly never come to you hat in hand before, but there's always a first time and this is it."

Janet looked at her in surprise. "Why Hetty," she said, "whatever are you talking about?"

Hetty hesitated. Janet was being coy, that's all. Well, Hetty would be direct and get it over with. Then it came to her in a flash. She would let Janet name Sara's punishment, that was it! Janet had raised a parcel of children, surely she could come up with something original. Taking a deep breath, Hetty announced, "No point beating around the bush, Janet. You know very well that Sara punched Felix in the nose and drew blood."

"Oh, for heaven's sake, Hetty," laughed Janet, "calm down. Felix explained everything. Sara didn't punch him at all."

"*What?*" said Hetty, stunned.

"Felix said they were just playing," said Janet mildly. "He said it was an accident."

Felix looked away, far away, towards the barn.

Hetty stared at Janet. "But...that can't be. I saw her do it with my own eyes! She's become a wilful and deceitful little terror!"

"Nonsense," said Janet calmly, "I know Sara very well, and she couldn't possibly be a terror. It's just a stage. Children go through these things, and Sara Stanley is no exception. Would you care for some tea, Hetty?"

Hetty couldn't believe her ears. "A stage!" she exploded. "It's not just a stage. She's... transformed! I tell you, that girl is not herself."

"You can say that again," muttered Felix under his breath.

"Pardon?" said Janet.

"Uh...nothing," mumbled Felix, digging into his applesauce with a vengeance.

Janet turned to Hetty reassuringly. She placed a hand on Hetty's arm. "You mustn't overreact, Hetty dear. You've been a bundle of nerves lately. You must try to relax."

Hetty looked from Janet to Felix and back again, completely confused. "Relax?" she muttered. How on earth did they expect her to relax when everything was so completely jumbled? Things happened, then people told her they didn't happen. Sara acted like a little hellion and Janet King brushed it off as nonsense. Good Lord, had she lost her ability to think clearly?

Still, she reasoned, there was no point admitting failings to Janet, starting a turmoil of gossip in the family. Better to make light of it and deal with Sara in her own way.

"Well...perhaps I am a bit...rattled," she murmured vaguely to Janet. "I'll just wander home and have a nap after lunch."

"Lovely," said Janet, surprised that Hetty would accept even the smallest crumb of advice. "It'll do you the world of good."

Hetty cast Felix and his cotton-stuffed nose a piercing look, said her goodbyes and set off for Rose Cottage, with Janet's reassuring words rattling around her head. Sara only going through a stage? Good Lord, what sort of stage, and how long would it last? More to the point, how long would she herself last under these dreadful circumstances?

She began to panic at the thought of the future, Sara growing more uncontrollable, life at Rose Cottage becoming a horror, one big embarrassment, the whole town laughing because Hetty King couldn't control her own niece. Well, she sniffed, there were limits to everything, and she for one was not going sit back and allow Sara to walk all over her. No young whippersnapper was going to rule the roost while Hetty King had a drop of fight left in her body!

Striding ahead, she muttered aloud to the nodding grass, "Enough is enough!" Shaking her fist at the wind, which was threatening to blow off her hat, she declared, "If I don't put a stop to it soon, that child will drive me clear out of my mind!"

The fact was, if anyone had seen Hetty King all alone in the field, babbling and shaking her fist, they would have presumed that Sara had already accomplished the task very nicely.

Jo Pitts sat at the kitchen table wolfing down her meal. Her face smeared with butter, she held a cob of corn in either hand, munching one and then the other, then slurping, wiping her face with her sleeve and letting out a series of belches.

Hetty stood watching, her eyes widening with horror. "Gracious Providence, child, what has gotten into you?" she said through gritted teeth. "Where are your manners!"

"You got any more o' these? They're real tasty," said Jo, hurling a chewed corn cob past

Hetty's ear. Hetty ducked, barely dodging the flying cob. It landed in the sink with a thud. "Bull's-eye!" crowed Jo, leaning back in the chair to emit the loudest, most disgusting belch it had ever been Hetty's misfortune to hear. In a flash, Hetty's hard-won restraint flew out the window.

"*Sara Stanley!*" she demanded. "Say excuse me!"

"You're excused," said Jo.

"Not me...*you!*" retorted Hetty. "You're the one who regurgitated."

"No, I didn't, I burped," said Jo, digging bits of corn cob from her teeth with a grimy fingernail, then blithely flicking the offending sliver of cob onto Hetty's spanking clean floor.

"*Sara Stanley!*" said Hetty, aghast.

"Burpin' ain't a sin," said Jo. "Didn't ya never hear 'God Save our Burp'?"

Hetty paused, confused. "I beg your pardon?"

"I'll sing it for ya." Waving a corn cob in the air, Jo then bellowed 'God Save our Gracious King,' substituting a loud burp each time the word "King" came up.

Hetty froze. For the first time in her life she was utterly and totally speechless, and only a flush of red creeping up her neck and into her face belied the fact that her blood was boiling. Hetty King was having a full-fledged fit of apoplexy; still, she summoned up every ounce of control she could muster and said quietly, "Sara dear. Remember when I said I was sorry? Remember how I said I would try my best with you?"

Jo nodded, rolling another cob of corn in butter.

Hetty continued, in honeyed tones. "I see now that, in spite of my efforts, all the good intentions in the world might not be enough. And so, Sara dear, that is why I must ask you to go to the sink."

"The sink?" muttered Jo. "What for?"

"Because I am asking you to. Do as I say just this once, dear," Hetty murmured sweetly.

Annoyed, Jo pushed back her chair and swaggered over to the sink. "Don't tell me I have to wash my hands *again*?"

"Oh no," cooed Hetty. "Not your hands, dear. *Your mouth*." With that, she grabbed Jo

Pitts in a hammerlock and lathered up a bar of soap.

"Quit it, ya old battle-ax!" hollered an astounded Jo, twisting from her grasp and ducking behind the kitchen table. Hetty leaped after her and they faced each other like cornered tigers, each waiting for the other to make a move. Then Jo made a sudden leap to the right and Hetty sprang to the left. They raced round and round the table, Hetty trying to grab hold of the girl, until they were both gasping and out of breath.

"When I catch you, I'm going to teach you a lesson you'll never forget!" promised Hetty as she lunged across the table to head Jo off. Dishes and glassware crashed, shards flying every which way as Hetty slid over the table, seizing Jo Pitts by the neck and dragging her back to the sink.

Jo sputtered and struggled as Hetty grabbed the wet soap and vigorously washed out the girl's mouth with suds.

"There!" she said triumphantly as iridescent bubbles foamed from Jo's mouth. "That's what you get for using foul language around here!"

Suddenly Jo sprang away, and with a bloodcurdling war cry, she jammed the soap in Hetty's mouth. "AGGGAGAAHH" burbled Hetty as Jo Pitts laughed in her face and then raced for the door.

Hetty chased her, but Jo was too nimble. "See ya at school, Aunt Hetty!" she yelled.

Hetty chased her across the field until she stumbled and fell over a tree stump. Hetty went sprawling, frustrated, outraged and trembling, with great gobs of soapy bubbles foaming from her lips.

Chapter Thirteen

"We're here!" Sara shrieked with delight, racing down the gangway to be the first passenger off the boat. "Isn't it wonderful to be in a city?"

Gus looked around at the tumult of activity on the dock—the sailors hauling crates, the hawkers of vegetables, the passengers struggling with steamer trunks and tickets and crying children, the lot of them dodging horses and buggies and bicycles careening every which way. There was even an organ-grinder with a screeching monkey that scrambled and yanked at the legs of nicely dressed tourists in the hopes of begging a coin or two.

Try as he might, Gus couldn't figure out what in tarnation attracted Sara to all of this noise and commotion. Not for him the crowds and the hustle and bustle, folks running here and there, always frazzled, too busy to shake a fellow's hand and give him a friendly hello!

Sara, on the other hand, was enchanted with the exciting sights and sounds of the port. She watched with interest as sailors hoisted crates from the holds of ships whose foreign flags snapped smartly in the breeze. She admired all the well-dressed passengers disembarking with their children and maids and luggage, imagining all sorts of fascinating destinations and conjuring up imaginary adventures for all of them.

"See that man?" she whispered, pointing out a gentleman with a great handlebar moustache and a malacca cane. "He's dangerous. I bet he's a mysterious secret agent on his way to conduct an investigation into a double murder."

"Go on with ya," laughed Gus. "He's most likely an old grandpa come to visit his gran'children."

"And that lady with the funny hat, the one with the feathers," said Sara, "she is a great star of the theater fresh from a command performance for the King of England, where he got down on bended knee and begged her to be Queen. I wonder if she said yes! I must go and ask for her autograph!"

"You will not!" said Gus. "She'll think you're crazy. I didn't come all this way to pester ladies for their names on a piece o' paper. I come to find Captain Crane, remember?"

"You have no romance in your soul, Gus Pike," complained Sara, dawdling behind him to admire the deep red fire of the sunset. Gus, however, was not to be distracted by sunsets, nor by Sara's flights of fancy. Totally preoccupied with his mission to find his friend Captain Crane, he hurried her forward along the dock.

Ahead lay the city, its roofs and spires dim in a shroud of violet smoke. To their right lay the harbor, taking on tints of copper and deep rose as it stretched out towards the sunset. A fine, gray mist was beginning to roll in. Far off, Sara could see a lighthouse, the watchful eye of its beacon flaring through the gathering fog.

With a pang, Sara thought of the lighthouse at Avonlea and the wonderful starlit evenings she and Felix and Felicity had once spent there as Gus showed them how to tend the light. She glanced quickly at Gus to see if he had the same thoughts, but he was approaching a sailor who was unloading a crate from a winch.

"Hello there, mate," said Gus. "We just got off that ship over there and I was wonderin' if ya might know of a street called Twister Lane."

The sailor scratched his head thoughtfully. "Nope. Can't say as I do. Hey Bud," he called out to a burly old sailor who was lighting up a pipe for an evening smoke. "Fella here wants to know where Twister Lane be."

The sailor took a deep drag on his pipe and eyed Gus greedily. "Ain't in the business of givin' out information for free, lad."

Gus reached in his pocket, pulled out a quarter and placed it in the old man's out-stretched hand. The old fellow looked down at the coin ruefully. Two bits? Ya get what ya pays for, he muttered to himself. "Head out there and follow yer nose," he said, pointing inland. "Ya can't miss it."

It was pitch dark, a suffocating darkness trapped inside drifts of pea soup fog. Gus and Sara had been plodding wearily up and down twisting, mist-shrouded streets for what seemed like hours. Luckily Gus had brought a lantern from home to light the way, but the further they walked, the thicker the fog became, and the darker and dingier the streets.

They had long since lost their way after stumbling through one filthy alley after another. The fog billowed in on gusts of wind; they made wrong turns; streets vanished as if by magic in the mist. Their lantern cast only a pale, dusty glow that failed to penetrate the murkiness. For all they knew, by now they were walking in circles.

"Guess I should'a given that old man more'n a quarter," said Gus. "We been fol- lowin' our noses for an awful long time." He waved the lantern around. "Thing of it is, I can barely find my nose, let alone the sign o' the Black Parrot." He glanced down at Sara. "You gettin' hungry?" he asked, suddenly remembering that they had polished off the last of Felicity's chicken sandwiches on the ship much earlier in the day.

Sara was famished and her stomach was gurgling loudly, but she was determined not to utter a word of complaint lest Gus think she was a whiner and a weakling. Gritting her teeth, she muttered, "Oh no, I'm just fine. Couldn't eat a thing."

"Too bad," said Gus, "cuz I'm starvin', myself. I was hopin' we could find a place to grab a bite o' supper, but if you're not hungry, then…"

Sara bit her lip. "Well…I could manage something small, if you insist," she said, trying not to appear overly eager. Not only was she hungry enough to eat a horse, her shoes were pinching unmercifully and she was bone-tired, as weary as she had ever been in her life.

She sighed longingly. A bed, any bed, would feel like heaven right now! That and a steaming cup of hot chocolate, the kind Aunt

Hetty made for her every night. No, she corrected herself hastily, forget Aunt Hetty. It was far better to do without hot chocolate if Hetty King came with it.

Sara was shivering now. The night air was chilly, but she had left Avonlea so impulsively that she hadn't even thought of the weather. Hugging her sweater around her shoulders, she kept silent, trodding dutifully along beside Gus and conjuring up images of a chair pulled up to a cozy fire, of toast slathered with butter and jam, roast beef with crispy brown potatoes and sweet apple pudding, steamy-hot and fresh from the oven. She was mentally devouring a gorgeous freshly baked plum cake smothered under layers and layers of whipped cream when she heard a creaking sound.

"Gus," she said, "listen. There's something over there…"

"Where?" said Gus.

She whirled about. She could hear his voice, a hollow echo, but she couldn't see him.

"Gus, where are you?" she called out. Now there was no answer. "*Gus!*" she yelled, her voice rising in panic only to melt into the fog.

A hand suddenly reached out and touched her. She screamed and then breathed a sigh of relief when Gus spoke to her, close by her side.

"Nothin' to be scared of, Sara," he said with a laugh. "I'm right here."

"Thank goodness," she gasped. "For a minute I thought I'd lost you!" The creaking sound drifted towards her again. "Listen Gus..." she said, standing stock-still. "There it is again. Can you hear it?"

He froze, listening intently. The creaking grew louder. "Yep," he said, reaching through the fog towards the sound. His hand touched metal. Moving closer, he held up the lantern, straining to see.

"Well, I'll be darned!" He laughed. "Will you have a look at that."

Sara peered into the mist where the pale lantern light illuminated an iron bracket grinding eerily in the wind. A rough wooden sign was attached to the bracket, carved in the ghostly shape of a bird. On it was painted in barely legible letters "The Black Parrot."

"Ya led me straight to it!" said Gus, happily. "Thanks a million, Sara. I never would'a found it without you!" His hand moved along the wall. "There's gotta be a door here somewhere…"

"Maybe we should wait for morning," said Sara in a small voice.

"What for?" whispered Gus, inching along the wall in the dark, feeling for a doorway. "We're here, we come all this way to find the sign o' the Black Parrot, why wait?"

"I don't know. This place…it's so quiet. I don't like it, Gus." Sara felt a shiver creeping up her spine.

"Look Sara, we ain't sure where we are," Gus pointed out reasonably. "If we take off now, who knows if we'll find it again? Besides, I know it ain't a palace, but I betcha Captain Crane's expectin' us. Most likely he's got a big pot o' stew cooked up, just waitin' for us to pop in." Gus stopped short. "Hey, I think I found a door."

He lifted a rusted latch and pushed. The door gave way and groaned open. He stepped inside to find pitch darkness. The air smelled foul. He heard the flutter of wings and ducked down. A bat? He swallowed hard and then whispered to Sara, "Something's fishy. Better wait outside."

"Gus no...don't go in!" pleaded Sara.

"Shhh," whispered Gus. "Do as I say."

He handed her the lantern and, putting his finger to his lips as a warning, he stepped inside the dark hovel.

The door creaked shut.

Sara stood alone, frozen with fear. The fog billowed around her like a gray cloak. The lantern cast a yellowish glow around her, but except for that faint circle of light, she might as well have been lost on the surface of the moon. Her heart pounded like a trip-hammer as she strained to listen. There was only silence.

Inside the hovel, Gus took one careful step at a time. A bat swooped by him. His arms went up defensively and he cried out.

From out of the gloom, a voice answered. "Come in, my boy. I been waitin' for ye."

"Captain Crane?" Gus said excitedly, a huge grin spreading from ear to ear. "Is that you?"

He heard the scratch of a match. Then a flame flickered as it lit a candle. There, in the murky half-light shed by the candle, was Abe

Pike, a great ugly scar creasing his face from forehead to chin.

"Pa!" cried Gus in horror, backing swiftly towards the door and flinging it open. "It's a trap! Run, Sara. RUN!"

Sara took one look and caught a horrible glimpse of Abe Pike, then of Gus, his eyes widening with fear. "Gus!" she screamed. Too late. Abe lunged for him.

"No, ya don't!" yelled Abe, his muscular arms around Gus's neck, dragging him back into the shack and kicking the door shut in Sara's face.

She stood there frozen to the spot, terrified. From within the shack, she heard Gus scream again, "RUN, SARA!"

In a flash she dropped the lantern and backed away, stumbling into the gutter. The door to the shack flew open and Abe Pike peered out into the billowing fog. He held a knife, its blade gleaming. He picked up the lantern she had dropped and held it out, the weak circle of light swinging back and forth in an arc. Trembling she ducked down, soaking her dress in the filthy gutter. When he couldn't find her, he swore loudly and slammed the door shut.

Trembling, freezing with cold, Sara crawled to her feet and fled, racing blindly into the fog. Gus's words pounded in her ears. She could hear the sound of her heart thudding. Tears streamed down her face and her breath came in short gasps as she raced through twisted alleys.

The pea soup fog enveloped her. She fell, tearing her dress and scraping up against a wall that loomed up out of nowhere. Blood streamed from a cut to her face as she stumbled ahead screaming, "Help! Police! Somebody help!"

Far off she heard the rumble of wagon wheels and fled towards the sound. She prayed she was running in the right direction, that Abe Pike wouldn't harm Gus. She thought of the sharp blade of the knife gleaming in the fog and she ran even faster, her heart thudding.

Suddenly, in the shadows, she saw something move. A claw of a hand reached out from the mist and hovered there. She stifled a scream, then almost sobbed with relief as the fog shifted. The hand belonged to a ragged, bearded old man who was moving slowly towards her.

"Oh, please help me, sir, " she cried out, "I must find a constable, I must…"

The words caught in her throat as she realized he couldn't possibly help her. There were frightening, vacant hollows where his eyes were supposed to be. Mumbling incoherently, he shuffled towards her, unseeing, his bird-like hands groping through the fog. "Penny for the poor, penny and porridge, spare a penny for the poor." He caught her wrist and cackled madly, "Caught one, I did!"

She wrenched herself away and fled, the sound of his laughter resounding into the night. Terrified, she tore down one twisted alley after another, finally emerging onto a narrow, mist-shrouded lane, where her heart leaped with joy at familiar sounds.

She could hear dogs barking and the neighing of horses, the rattle of buggy wheels! They were close. She could make out the gleam of lantern light now, the shape of dark horses, the clatter of hooves heading in her direction. Surely the driver would see her, hear her!

Thrilled, she ran forward in front of the oncoming buggy, waving her hands, yelling as loudly as she could, "Stop, please stop!"

To her horror, instead of slowing down, the driver was whipping the horses even faster. The buggy was careening down the alley straight for her. Then, with seconds to spare, she dodged the flying hooves and went sprawling in the mud, shocked and panic-stricken. Dogs barked viciously in the shadows. A couple of mangy curs, their teeth bared, crept towards her, snarling.

Scrambling backwards, she crawled to her feet as the dogs loped warily around her, their growls menacing. She had to find someplace to hide—a door, a cellar, anything! To her horror, the street suddenly ended in a brick wall. She whirled around, terrified. The dogs were almost upon her. Her heart in her mouth, she dug a toehold in the wall. A dog leaped. Sharp teeth ripped her dress, pulling her back, but she kicked and twisted free and sprang up, nails digging into the wall. Up, up she climbed, and summoning strength she never knew she possessed, she hurled herself over to the other side.

She landed face down, sinking in a heap of foul-smelling garbage, arms flailing, struggling to breathe.

It flashed through her mind that she would suffocate in this filth and muck, she would die, nobody would ever find her! The dogs were yelping wildly on the other side of the wall. She was gasping for breath when a hand seized her and yanked her to her feet.

Sara looked up, sputtering, into a heavily pock-marked face. He was a slimy ruffian, his hair dank and stringy. A narrow-brimmed hat shadowed cat eyes that were slits, glittering yellowish green in the dark. He lifted her roughly by the collar and dangled her like a fish on a hook.

"Jo Pitts!" he sneered. "I got a score to settle with you!"

His hand clamped tightly over her mouth, muffling her screams. He dragged her with him as she kicked and struggled in vain. In moments, the two had disappeared into the night, swallowed up in dense billows of fog.

TO BE CONTINUED

❦   ❦   ❦

Will Aunt Hetty survive the *new* and
not-so-improved Sara Stanley?

Will the real Sara Stanley have to pay
the price for Jo Pitts' crimes?

Find out in DOUBLE TROUBLE,
the second half of this two-book adventure.